BODY CHA

CW00547837

HUNTER DAVIES was born in Johnstone, F
ated from University College, Durham,
journalist. His first novel, *Here We Go, Round the Mulberry Bush* (1965),
was adapted for a major feature film. In 1968, Davies published the only
authorised biography of the Beatles, entitled *The Beatles*; the book remains
in print. He followed his first novel with four others, the last of which was
Body Charge (1972), before turning his efforts to non-fiction writing. His
book *The Glory Game* (1972) is regarded as one of the best books ever
written about football and is still in print today. He has continued to write
prolifically over the years and has published books in a variety of genres,
including several series of children's novels and a number of biographies.
As a journalist, he still writes a column in the *New Statesman* (on football)
and in the *Sunday Times* (on money). He and his wife, Margaret Forster,
also a writer, live in London.

HUNTER DAVIES

BODY CHARGE

WITH A NEW INTRODUCTION BY THE AUTHOR

VALANCOURT BOOKS

Body Charge by Hunter Davies
First published London: Weidenfeld and Nicolson, 1972
First Valancourt Books edition 2013

Published by Valancourt Books, Kansas City, Missouri
Publisher & Editor: JAMES D. JENKINS
20th Century Series Editor: SIMON STERN, University of Toronto
http://www.valancourtbooks.com

Library of Congress Cataloging-in-Publication Data

Davies, Hunter, 1936-
  Body charge : a novel / by Hunter Davies ; with a new
introduction by the author. – First Valancourt Books edition.
    pages ; cm. – (20th century series)
  ISBN 978-1-939140-36-4 (*acid free paper*)
  I. Title.
PR6054.A883B63 2013
823'.914–dc23

                        2013009341

Cover photograph © Shutterstock.com
Set in Dante MT 11/13.5

INTRODUCTION

I HAVE NO MEMORY of writing this novel. I know that sounds inverted showing off, but it's truth. In fact I can hardly remember that I did used to write novels. Must have been someone else using my name. Or typewriter. Remember them? Inky, clattery things.

It was a long time ago, in what now appears to have been another country. Like teenagery, it all now seems foreign. I am sure if had to meet myself now, walking along as a teenager, I simply wouldn't recognize myself and would pass by on the other side, feeling sorry for him.

Now, I remember, I did start off writing novels, and started off so well my first one *Here We Go, Round the Mulberry Bush* was bought by United Artists, a big U.S. film company. It was a very British sort of teenage film, with kipper ties and great Sixties music – and in Technicolor. That was a big thing, in 1966. My wife, around the same time, had her novel *Georgy Girl* made into a film – but it was black and white. That was looked upon as arty. Colour was vulgar, especially if it featured kipper ties and teenagers.

I then did four other novels – *Body Charge* being the fifth. I was always starting off in great style, great energy and excitement, laughing at all my own jokes, and then about halfway I would stop and think, hmm, plot, I'll have to think of a plot, quick, what can I do, where can I get a plot from?

With *Body Charge*, I do remember thinking if I have a murder, surely that will give me a plot. Easy. So off I zoomed. But where I got to, God knows. Until yesterday, picking it up again after 42 years, I really could remember nothing about the contents.

But I can remember being well pleased with the title. It was a sort of three-way pun. 'Body charge' is a football term, when you barge into someone, knock them off the ball. It can apply to someone selling their body, like a male or female prostitute. And it sounds sort of criminal, up on a bodily harm charge.

I do know I was mad on football at the time, still am, but too old and knackered to play it. Back in 1970, still in my early thirties, I was playing football all the time on Hampstead Heath, like the hero in the novel. Until I opened the book again, I had forgotten he was a mini cab driver, a rather camp one, and I had forgotten all the characters.

I see that the novel is dedicated to Richard Simon. He was my agent, still alive and well, retired and living in Edinburgh. He was gay, and I got to know some of his boy friends, and was fascinated by them and their world and language. I felt pretty smart using the phrase 'all who cruise with it', an expression not known by the general public at the time.

It had only been since the 1967 Sexual Offences Act that homosexual behaviour between consenting adults had ceased to be illegal in England and Wales, so it was all sort of new and exciting, with people beginning slowly to come out and not just out, but flaunting, but of course for the vast majority of the population, and for gay people, it was still not talked about or admitted.

In my 1968 biography of the Beatles, I wanted to explain that Brian Epstein was gay and that one reason he was attracted to the Beatles was because he fancied John – who wasn't gay. Brian was masochistic in that he was attracted to butch boys, who usually beat him up. In the book, I did manage to describe him as a 'gay bachelor', another phrase not in public use at the time – which was fortunate as his mother Queenie, who denied Brian was homosexual anyway, did not object to the phrase.

I suppose these strands were in my head when I was writing the novel. People did start to pretend to be camp, such as my hero, or claimed to be bisexual, but of course there was still fierce homophobia. There had been an incident of gay bashing on Hampstead Heath, in fact in various parts of the UK, as the so-called skinhead working-class gangs took it out on the small minority of gays who were coming out of the closet.

I started reading the novel again, without remembering any of the characters, but knowing that a murder was going to happen. And do you know – I could not put it down! Well, for the first 100 pages I was laughing aloud, proud of my own jokes and smart remarks, enjoying the main characters, thinking they were smartly drawn and fairly typical of the times.

Not a lot of it had dated too much, apart from prices and references to British TV stars and shows of the time. The joke about Twiggy – managing to be successful with no breasts, making a girl think she will be successful with no height – still makes sense, as Twiggy is still well known. But of course I would never make such a sexist, bad taste remark today, wash your mouth out, Hunter.

When the plot starts in earnest, I got a bit lost. My fault really. I am slow on the uptake, can never follow crime dramas on TV. But it does seem awfully clever and well worked out. I am sure you will follow it all, being smart, and enjoy it.

I was amazed, looking through my cuttings files, to discover that it did get some good reviews, and quite a lot of them. The lit pages did seem to treat it as a proper novel and me as a proper novelist, which I never did. I always felt a fraud. I could do half a novel, have fun, keep it moving, pacey and funny and contemporary, make you want to read on, then it seemed to become such a worry.

I gave up fiction after *Body Charge* and concentrated instead on non-fiction, going on to do around 40 non-fiction books—biographies, travel, social history, and stuff. It seemed easier. When you get stuck with non-fiction, you can always go out and do some more research, interview someone, get copy from somewhere. With fiction, it really has to come out of your head.

But reading this again now, I think I might well go back to novels. As long as I can keep it fun, the observations sharp, characters clear, making serious points but with a light touch, and don't worry too much about tying things up. Life doesn't tie things up anyway . . .

Hunter Davies
London

March 26, 2013

BODY CHARGE

For Richard Scott Simon Ltd
and all who cruise with it

I

There was an Inspector watching me. I hadn't seen him at first. I'd been parked for about ten minutes, combing my hair in the mirror, admiring my winter tan, pulling down my eyelids to see if I was anaemic and going through my Yoga finger exercises. I was too early for the Glasgow train and Euston was almost empty, which was most unusual. I'd taken Joff to catch the Birmingham train and now I was about to do what Mr Innocent said I should do. I'd never tried it before and I was very nervous. Mr Innocent could carry anything off but I felt very conspicuous. Perhaps I shouldn't have put on my seersucker shirt. I'd tried to speak to three people already, pulling down my window and going pisst, but they'd all rushed off in terror as if I'd made an indecent proposal.

The Inspector had moved up and was standing right beside me. I could see the hairs in his nostrils in my driving mirror. When mine get to that length I always cut them. Then I could see his shoes, all slushy and soggy with standing around in the snow. If he'd been a common or garden policeman he'd have had on good strong common or garden boots. I waited for him to tap on my window and ask me to step out. I looked at my watch. As he walked across in front of the car bonnet to get to my door, I moved to the passenger side, threw open the door and jumped out. I rushed into the Euston concourse shouting 'Not to worry. I'm coming. Cooo-eeee! It's me . . .'

If the Inspector followed me, I'd be for it. As I turned, fearing that he was on my tail, three air hostesses followed by two air stewards came down the stairs from the new posh waiting lounge. The girls looked beautiful and cool and highly superior, stuck in an old-fashioned place like a railway station when by nature they should be above us all in the clouds. The two stewards were saying cheerio to the girls, best of luck, be good, then they stood alone, exchanging looks. They had polished chins, the sort which take three shaves a day to keep clean, tight mouths and even tighter little arses. I knew the type.

'Want some cheap transport?' I blurted out to them, puffing and panting, but trying to look smart and fast. I'd been trying to look smart and fast all day, all week in fact. It was part of my new persona. I'd given up all that introversion stuff.

'No thanks,' said one, walking quickly away. 'Certainly not,' said the other. Their little arses bounced away, all prim and proper, heading for the exit. That's the worst of taking on a part. When you get snubbed, it hurts more. At least when I'm serious and all worried and self-conscious I'm always ready for what's going to happen. Such as nothing.

They had both suddenly stopped and were looking at each other. One of them turned, waiting for me to catch up, watching me carefully.

'How cheap?'

'Anywhere in the West End, fifty p.,' I said, grabbing their little overnight cases. 'Quick, follow me. I'm just outside. The black Cortina. My name's Franko. Don't forget.'

I left them standing, despite carrying their cases, and went racing back to the car. The Inspector was beside it, smirking, his arm on the roof as if I was Nobby Ludd and he'd just spotted me and was claiming his £5. I threw up the boot of the car and started to put the cases in.

'Just a minute,' he said, his hand on my shoulder.

'These bloody air stewards,' I said, shaking him off and pretending to ignore him. I hate being touched. 'They keep me waiting every time.' I stood back, as if I'd just noticed him. 'You what?'

'I said just a minute. You were touting for business, weren't you? I saw you here last week.'

'Not me, Inspector. I was in Portugal, wasn't I.'

'Just watch it. Which firm do you work for?'

I handed him the hand-out card, the one meant for handing out. 'Fantastic Cabs, Prop. H. Innocent. London Airport a Speciality.'

I could see the two stewards at last, emerging from the station, staring round looking for me. I waved at them and shouted, opening the doors for them to get in.

'Excuse me, pleeese,' I said to the Inspector, trying to move him to one side so that I could get on with my right and proper employment. I was making as much show as possible, shepherding them in, giving them the full treatment.

'And your licence,' said the Inspector, holding out his hand.

I sighed and handed it over, apologising to the stewards for keeping them waiting, normal service would be resumed as soon as possible, please extinguish your safety belts. Once I get going, there's no stopping me.

The Inspector was examining the licence carefully while I did some heavy eyelid raising and deep sighing. It was a brand new licence. Mr Innocent had got it for me himself. My old one had been rather nasty and six months out of date, what with being away and all that. I'd never liked the hieroglyphics on it anyway, such as Wigan Magistrates' Court. Speeding £15. This one was rather attractive.

'What's the matter, Franko?' said one of the stewards, popping his head out. 'Isn't it super, Franko always meeting us,' said the other, perfectly in tune.

'Oh, so you know this gentleman, do you,' said the Inspector.

'Bloody hell, it's a standing order, isn't it,' I said, butting in, just in case they got too confident and got ahead of me with their story. 'Every time they land at Manchester I have to come and pick them up here. Don't I?'

'Wouldn't be the same without you, Franko.'

'Are you sure you didn't just pick them up *now*?' said the Inspector, weakening, but trying one last attempt.

'They phoned the office from Manchester, as usual,' I said. 'Check with Mr Innocent. It's all in the book.'

Three black cabs had stopped in front and the drivers had got out and were watching me. If I got away from the Inspector safely, I'd probably get their boot in my balls. The two stewards looked good for a giggle but not for a brawl in the gutter. Mr Innocent himself, no less, had been attacked the previous week by two taxi drivers. I didn't want my delicate features ruined by a gang of roughs. Something exciting, perhaps. But not two uncouth taxi drivers.

'You better watch your step, that's all,' said the Inspector, slowly stepping aside. 'You know the laws. No soliciting. OK?'

'That's what you think, ducky,' I said, closing the door quickly so that he couldn't hear me. The two stewards giggled, not really knowing what was going on but lapping up all my insolence.

The Inspector was talking to two constables who had appeared and were also watching me, stepping into the road, trying to recognise me or the car. If they'd been there earlier to witness the Inspector's pathetic performance, he might have been forced to have come on stronger. I drove away quickly, swerving to avoid them.

'You are a mini-cab, aren't you,' said one of the stewards. 'You're not going to do something awful to us and we'll both wake up in Buenos Aires.' They both giggled.

'What would you fancy?' I said.

'Oooh, that's up to you.'

They were holding hands on the back seat, sliding gradually into being themselves now that they were back home in London and not forced to stride manfully up and down the aisles giving out duty-free whisky in a deep voice.

They wanted to go to the William IV in Hampstead, which was lucky for me, being so near home. They invited me in for a snifter, insisting I should come with them, have a meal afterwards perhaps, go on and do something exciting. I'd gone off them already. They'd done me a good turn, but they thought I'd meant it all. Give those sort of people any encouragement and you've had it. They're so desperate, really, so open, so eager, once they think you're on their side. I made an excuse and left them, saying I had to get home to my wife and seven kids.

I headed straight for Fantastic, hoping Mr Innocent and Midge would be there so that I could give them a blow-by-blow account of my very first success. Midge never managed a pick-up for his return journey. He was always full of excuses, about the police watching, or the station or the airport being absolutely empty. He was scared, really, and secretly hoped that one day Mr Innocent would be caught. Mr Innocent was the world expert. His car was never empty. Wherever he was, at whatever time of the day or night, he always managed to solicit business and find someone waiting to be taken somewhere. That was how he'd found me.

I'd been standing at London Airport in a mental fog, trying to work out all the things that had happened while I'd been away, such as who was this bloke Giro and what did a decimal coin look like. Mr Innocent had me by the arm before I knew what had happened. He had a funny armband on and looked like an air-port official. He asked if I had anything to declare and I said yes, lots, and immediately he steered me to a green exit which clearly said Nothing to Declare. I protested but he put his hand over my mouth and told me to shut up. We were straight through, with him marching ahead as if he owned the place, and I was in his cab before I knew where I was.

All the way home he'd moaned non-stop about the trouble he had getting good drivers. They were all Irish and he hated the Irish. I said I was a fantastic driver. He said that was the name of his firm. Why didn't I join him. I only needed to work when I felt like it. Just mornings would do. It was a lovely life. He would knit another arm-band for me if I was a good boy and didn't tell anyone.

I hadn't been thinking of becoming a mini-cab driver, though I'd decided I would have to get some sort of job. I wanted something where I wouldn't get involved. I'd had enough of being involved. I wanted something where I would be my own boss, make my own hours, keep myself to myself. It was beginning to look as if Fantastic might suit me very well.

I could see that both Midge and Mr Innocent were in the office when I got back. I slammed out of the car, rushing across the street to tell them about my big success with the air stewards. As I got to the door I could hear Mr Innocent screaming and shouting at Midge. They were standing one behind the other with Sparkle in the middle, holding her delicate hands to her delicate ears, pretending she'd never heard obscene language before.

Everyone always stood one behind the other at Fantastic. It wasn't for protection, backs to the wall, here comes Franko, though all week I'd had to put up, as usual, with that sort of joke, once they heard my surname was Baxter. It was because Fantastic's office was not an office but a scruffy little corridor, sandwiched between a caff on one side and a surgical appliance store on the other. Some hardboard had been stretched across the top to make a roof, a glass door had been put at the front and overnight the alleyway had become the London headquarters of Fantastic Limited, Nation-Wide Mini-Cabs.

I said hello all, but nobody answered. Midge stood silently, peering at me. Midge never said anything. He was tall and thin with pebble specs and very high cheek bones. Something extraordinary would have had to happen for Midge to have answered back for once. He was called Midge because he was so tall. I found him rather sinister.

Mr Innocent was chuntering on, blaming Midge for whatever he'd done or not done. Mr Innocent had no nickname because Mr Innocent suited him so much.

He was eighteen stone and not much more than five foot high. He was one complete ball of fat and it was impossible to tell where his legs finished and his stomach began. Yet his face had the most beautiful texture, smooth and round and angelic. His eyes sparkled and he was always laughing. Meeting him face to face you would have trusted him with your life's savings. But his body was a shambles. His one suit was always scruffy and his fingers black with nicotine.

But the thing which attracted me to Mr Innocent from the beginning was not his awful fatness nor his cherubic face but his beautiful, shoulder-length hair. He looked after it lovingly, shampooing it every night. I don't know whether someone had started to bring him up-to-date, and then had suddenly stopped at his hair, or he'd just got it into his head that to be in fashion all he needed to do was grow his hair. Whatever the reason, it didn't suit him. In fact he looked grotesque. A middle-aged Billy Bunter trying to look like Tiny Tim. I know I can't talk, poncing about at thirty in teenage fashions, but for Mr Innocent at fifty to pick upon one thing and then take it to extreme was magnificent in its awfulness.

He sat down at last, mopping his brow, but still swearing at Midge. 'Tea, I must have tea,' he started bleating, kicking Sparkle to go and get him some. 'Gawd, why do I waste my time shouting! You know what my ticker's like.' Then he started laughing, his high-pitched gurgling laugh, convulsed at the thought of having another heart attack.

I found Mr Innocent very funny, whether he was telling us the details of his latest heart attack or how he was going to sue the Minister of Transport. But I feared that if I told my friends to come and see him, just ring up for a cab, he's a scream, they might not find him as hysterical as I did. They might decide he was simply a fat little con man.

Sparkle was even smaller than Mr Innocent, well under five feet high, and was the only person who could stand sideways in the office at the same time as Mr Innocent. She had been chosen for her height, not her intelligence. When it came to efficiency, she was useless. If any casual driver didn't turn up when Mr Innocent had asked for them, they could always blame Sparkle and get away with it.

She had her mirror out and was lost in careful examination of her eyes. Sparkle lived in a dream world where people were constantly about to discover her. She was absolutely confident it was going to happen. Twiggy had done it with no breasts. Sparkle was going to do it with no height, not to mention all the other things she hadn't got. She'd decided that it was her eyes which were particularly special. As she studied them anxiously for signs, Mr Innocent grabbed the mirror from her hand and told her again to get him some tea.

'Anyway, Midge,' said Mr Innocent, caressing his hair in Sparkle's mirror. 'I gave strict instructions that the Hilltop job was not to be paid for.'

Midge groaned. Mr Innocent was going back to the argument.

'Mrs Guttings asked me specially,' he continued. 'She wanted none of her guests to pay. We're going to bill her later. And yet I find that you and Franko have taken pay from every guest. What the hell goes on here? And Christ, where's that cup of tea, Sparkle? What do I have to do to get attention, cut an artery?'

'You haven't given me no money,' said Sparkle, waiting for her mirror, to check that everything was still there.

'Bloody hell,' said Mr Innocent. 'Here I am at death's door and all she thinks about is money. Midge, make yourself useful instead of standing against the wall like a streak of shite.'

Midge slowly gave Sparkle some money. Mr Innocent had never

asked me for money, so far. Perhaps he thought he'd rescued me from the gutters by giving me a job. Perhaps with not having a suit, unlike Mr Innocent who was so proud of his awful suit, I must be very hard up. Or perhaps he really knew all about me and was saving himself up for one really big tickle.

'Midge told me that all Mrs Guttings' guests had to pay,' I said, very virtuous, stirring up trouble.

'That's what Boo told me,' said Midge, equally blameless.

'And Boo's left,' shouted Mr Innocent. 'Christ! You lot pass the buck quicker than a hot turd. God give me strength.'

I knew why Midge had made sure he'd got paid. He would never have seen his money otherwise. I'd already sussed that one of Mr Innocent's favourite tricks was to get people to send the money later, direct to him. The normal system was that each driver kept his fares, but paid a weekly sum to Mr Innocent, to cover the office expenses, Sparkle's pay, and Mr Innocent's commission for getting the jobs. Now and again, of course, if someone was having a party, you took everyone home and the host paid all the bills later to Mr Innocent. That's when the trouble began, getting your money back from Mr Innocent.

Mr Innocent launched into a long whine, all about us ruining his customer relations by not doing what Mrs Guttings had asked. It had taken him years to build up good customers, God knows, and then we came along, all greedy buggers, and spoiled everything. She'd be furious when she found out all her guests had paid. What were we worrying about anyway? He would have billed her later, then we would have got our money. Couldn't we trust him? Midge laughed. Sparkle sniggered. I whistled through my teeth.

'Ok then, I'll get a hold of Boo,' said Mr Innocent. 'I'll settle this once and for all. Where the hell is his phone number? And God, my bloody tea! Sparkle, I'm dying.' He grabbed hold of her and pushed her out of the door, then he turned to me. 'Now, Franko, I'll take that airport job. It's a return flight. I know them.'

'I know them,' I said. I didn't want him taking all the best jobs, now that I'd joined the big league and could find return pick-ups on my own.

'I know them better. You've got a lot to learn. And you said you wanted to finish early tonight, didn't you?'

'No I didn't.'

'I thought she wanted you home early?'

Mr Innocent must have been spying on me already. I had deliberately not mentioned any she, to anyone. But I wasn't going to play into his hands by arguing with him.

'I haven't done an airport yet,' I said. 'It could be £10, if I get a good pick-up.'

'*If* you get a pick-up,' he said, his belly rolling in mockery at my impudence. 'You young lads can't pick your nose, never mind pick up customers.'

That's another thing I liked about Mr Innocent. I was always a young lad.

2

I met Shuggy about a fortnight after I'd joined Fantastic. I was at Euston again, soliciting as usual for a return trip. He stood there looking so provincial and lost, so tall and innocent, with short hair, desperately carrying a brand new Adidas bag, trying to grasp some confidence from its dazzling whiteness. It was the bag which struck me first. He was so proud of it yet it seemed so out of character. He was walking up and down looking very worried, glancing at his watch, looking for someone yet trying not to look too hard unless something awful happened, like me coming up to him and saying 'Hello darling.' Which I did. It was just a joke. I couldn't help it. He ran straight for the Gents. His Mum must have warned him about people like me. Half way there, he changed track, suddenly realising that the Gents was the last place he should run to in such a situation.

I'd stopped and had gone to buy a *Standard* from the station stall before looking for some other likely customers. I'd spoiled that one by a cheap joke. As I came away from the stall, I came face to face with him again. He was asking for a *Sunday Post*.

'Can I carry your handbag?' I said, smiling at him. Having regretted the first remark, I was doing the same again. There are some people who for some reason push you into a character and having started it, you go on. He was the wrong person for camp jokes. He thought I meant them, which I did and I didn't. He was a nice lad. I was just chatting him up. He put his *Sunday Post* in his pocket, folding it in a square, the way workmen do on a building site, then he held his bag with both hands, glaring at me, guarding his virginity and whatever else he had inside.

'Piss off,' he said between his teeth. He'd heard about these cockneys and was determined from the beginning to put them in their place and let no one take advantage of him. But he couldn't really carry it off. His broad Glasgow accent made what little he said almost indecipherable.

'How's your Wee Wullie?' I asked. The bloke on the counter was watching me this time. 'You know,' I added hurriedly, 'the comic in the *Sunday Post*. My Granny used to read it. Or is it Oor Wullie? Come on, let's have a look.'

I grabbed the *Sunday Post* from his pocket before he knew what had happened and turned to the comic pages. Oor Wullie and the Broons looked exactly the same as I'd always remembered them. He stood looking at me, narrowing his eyes, trying to think of a suitable insult or whether to thump me once and for all.

'Have you come for a trial?' I asked him. It was a question out of the blue. He said yes before he had time to lie and keep me at bay. I told him I could tell he had. I often picked them up from the Northern trains on a Sunday afternoon. I took his bag and told him to follow me if he wanted a mini-cab.

He walked behind me, still suspicious, keeping a close watch on his bag. I prattled on, deciding to be serious and sensible this time. I asked him if he knew what Adidas stood for.

'Oh, is that how you pronounce it? I've taken it in visually on the tele but not verbally, if you know what I mean.'

He wasn't thick after all. I explained that it stood for Addi Dasler, Addi being short for Adolph. He was a German sports-goods manufacturer, now the biggest in the world. His brother had a rival firm called Puma.

'That's very in-ter-esting,' he said slowly, with only the slightest hint that he was mocking me.

We got to the car and I asked if it was Highbury or White Hart Lane. It was neither. He was going to Hendon United, the second-division club, one of the founder members of the Football League, but now a very draggy club. I didn't make any comment. They weren't a bad side. They had a few old stars who had played for the bigger clubs and had refused to leave London. Sometimes they discovered some good young players, but they never seemed to get a consistently balanced team to get back into the first division.

He sat in the back seat, bolt upright, looking out of the window, ready for anything. I hated passengers who sat in the back. That's for those awful taxi louts. People usually sit in the front in a mini-cab, which is always much more matey.

I asked him where he wanted to go and he said the club, and no messing about. I said he must be joking. There would be nobody there on a Sunday afternoon. He told me not to be so bloody clever. I had to do what I was told. We drove in silence for a while. I could tell he was thinking.

'Somebody was supposed to meet me at Euston,' he began slowly. 'Look, it's in this letter, February 22 . . .'

He leaned over to show it to me.

'February 22 is tomorrow,' I said. 'You're a day early.'

I didn't try to score at his expense, or tell him he'd made a stupid mistake. I just let him work it out. After a pause he said I had to carry on. Go straight to the club. Very obstinate, these Scottish lads.

We couldn't even get in the car park, it was all barricaded up. The ground was absolutely dead.

'Where to now, Squire?' I asked. That was one of Mr Innocent's favourite phrases. It irritated me when I heard him using it with people.

'I'm thinking,' said Shuggy.

He'd told me on the way to the ground that his name was Hugh Gallacher, much to his embarrassment. I said great. What an asset for a football player. He said no. It had always been a joke when people heard it. He stuck to Shug or Shuggy which he said was a common Glaswegian abbreviation for Hugh.

He'd been playing for a Scottish second-division club. They

hadn't been very successful but Shug had been leading goal-scorer, even though he was a winger. United had decided to look for a winger for a change, despite the trend away from them, especially one who could score. Shug didn't fancy his chances at all. They'd sent him a single ticket but he knew that after a couple of trials, he'd be back on the train to Glasgow.

'How much do I owe you?' he said, trying to open the back door. I told him not to be so daft. What was he going to do? He'd never been in London before, so how was he going to find his way round the wilds of Hendon on a rainy Sunday afternoon?

'Ok, clever cunt,' he said. 'What shall I do then?'

I told him to sit still and I'd make a phone call. I knew where one of the United players lived in Kentish Town, not far from me. I'd taken him to town the previous week. He lived with his Mum and she often had other young players staying with her.

I walked across the road to a telephone. The number wasn't in the directory and directory enquiries wouldn't give it to me either. A bloody second-division club landlady, going all exclusive. I tried the ex-directory operator and then the supervisor but they were both bitches and wouldn't tell me. I told them to get stuffed.

I'd come on so strong with Shug at first. Right from the beginning I'd been posing as a cockney man of the world and general smart-alec. Now I'd failed to help him, despite all my boastings.

I came back to the car and told him the phone was out of order. I said I knew where Mrs Pagan lived. I'd drive him there.

We drove in silence. I was regretting all my original bright chat. He seemed a nice lad, not half as provincial as I'd first imagined. Just lost. It was only now I was beginning to realise he'd been getting in a few digs at me. As a football fan, I genuinely wanted to know more about how Hendon had discovered him, how he felt, what he thought. I suppose I envied him, in a way. At eighteen, I never knew what I wanted to do. Still don't.

We got to Kentish Town and Mrs Pagan took him in at once. She pounced on the fact that the club hadn't met him at the station, without listening to the reasons why. She said it was disgusting, bringing the poor lad all that way. I pointed out it was Shuggy's mistake not the club's, but she wouldn't have it.

'I know what goes on up there. If you're in, you're in. If you're not, then they don't give a damn about you. Look at my Joey.'

'Oh shut up Mum,' said Joe, raising his head for a moment from the *People*.

Joe had heard of Shug and that he was due at the club for a trial. He said everybody had heard, what with him being called Hughie Gallacher and that. He was very friendly, considering that Shug was another rival for a place in the team. He got up and shook hands and said he'd show him to his room. He told Shug to ignore his mother. She was a bit Dullalypip. Shug smiled, pretending he'd heard the word before. He was obviously very relieved to find somewhere for the night and meet someone who knew who he was. It proved that he did exist and wasn't doomed to wandering round London with a strange mini-cab driver.

Shug went upstairs with Joe, forgetting about me. He didn't even say thanks. That's one thing about being a driver which I was just beginning to learn. You can be the most important person in the car, but when you come out into the real world, you have to take a back seat. But in a way that's an asset. You can see people in two lights, when they're keeping in with you and then when you're dismissed and no longer matter. It's in their reactions to the second set of circumstances that you get the most insight. Shug was obviously going to do well. He didn't look back.

'It really is disgusting what happens up there,' said Mrs Pagan. 'Did you see our Joe against Arsenal reserves? Smashing he was, really smashing. Everyone said so. *Hendon News*. Everyone. But the following week . . .'

She offered me some tea but I knew that meant listening to her memoirs. I noticed Shug's precious bag. He'd put it on the floor when he'd shaken hands with Joe. I thought about picking it up and taking it with me. Mrs Pagan was too busy nattering to notice. But I decided not to. My jokes hadn't gone down all that well. I left, forgetting completely that he hadn't paid me.

I met Zak one day coming back from Watford. I was doing seventy miles an hour on a motorway going in the direction of nowhere and getting there very quickly. I had no idea if I was facing North,

South, East or West. I was miles out with not a signpost in sight or a turning off. There was a bloke ahead, thumbing me like mad. I thought perhaps he'd been sent to tell me the way, as I'd been shouting so loudly. He was a hitch-hiker, which of course is illegal on a motorway. No wonder he was in a hurry to get off. He might know where he was going, or at least where I'd landed myself. So I stopped.

'Where you going?' I asked, as he got in.

'London,' he said.

'Where have you come from?'

'Amsterdam.'

'I see,' I said, smiling. As I drove away, a car I hadn't noticed before, which had been stationary near Zak, pulled away quickly and overtook us. The driver stared at me. I asked Zak if he knew who it was but he shook his head. Zak sat very still and content, at ease with himself and the world, very peaceful, doing nobody a favour, being neither grateful nor ungrateful. Just being himself. He had jeans and a cheap pair of blue painted plimsolls on. His face was a bit grey and spotty but his body was stocky, solid and relaxed. He smiled a lot but didn't appear to go in for much chat. When I'd been a hitch-hiker, in my youth, I'd always chatted like mad the second I got in the car, trying to pay my way by being bright and entertaining.

'Amsterdam, near Watford,' I said, trying to open him up.

'No. Amsterdam, Amsterdam.'

He smiled faintly, but a bit wearily. He'd met idiots before and, alas, they had to be tolerated, especially when they were giving you a lift.

'I've been hitch-hiking from Harwich. I took a dislike to the last lift. He said he was going to London but he wasn't. He made a grab for my flies, so I got out.'

'How disgusting,' I said.

'Not at all. It was his lying I didn't like.'

I thought about that remark all the way back to London. I went like the devil, speeding up motorways for miles, going as quickly as I could because if I was going the wrong way I'd find out quicker the faster I went. Then I'd go like hell all the way back again. Zak didn't seem to mind. He sat calmly, looking at nothing, letting it all hang out. He'd been to Amsterdam to learn to act, so he said. No, it wasn't an acting college. It was like an acting commune run by some rich Americans. He'd met one of them in Piccadilly one day who'd said come to Amsterdam and learn to act, all expenses paid. I tried to get more information about what had happened in Amsterdam, but he seemed bored. It's an age-gap thing, chatting up people. Under thirty they just don't care where you've come from, who you are, what you do, or even where you're going or what you're going to do next. You just are.

'Will you act here?' I said. 'National or Royal Shakespeare? You look a bit Royal Court to me.'

'No, I've learned to act,' he said, smiling.

'So what is it now? Underwater wrestling?' He laughed but didn't reply.

After a long silence, I said very suddenly, surprising almost myself, 'I'm a mini-cab driver.'

He said nothing. No applause, no cheers, no facetiousness, no comment. He hadn't asked one little thing about me, whether I like my eggs hard-boiled or soft-boiled or what colour underpants I had on, the really vital things that I'm always dying to know about people the minute I meet them.

'I said I'm a mini-cab driver.'

'Oh, I'm terribly sorry,' he suddenly said, looking very worried and apologetic, putting his hand on the door. 'I've no money. I'll get out now. I'm terribly sorry.' I wasn't sure if he was joking or not.

'Don't worry.'

'No, really. I must. It's your livelihood. I can't expect you to drive me for nothing.'

'Sit tight. Uncle Franko will look after you. I'm going to Tufnell Park anyway.' He sat back, satisfied, smiling to himself. It was like a complicated game, only he knew the rules and I didn't.

I'd discovered where he was going, but he wasn't quite sure of the street number. He'd only just moved there before he went away to Amsterdam, three months ago. I could drop him anywhere. He'd walk. He was used to walking.

'Don't your feet hurt in those shoes?'

'They're all I've got. I even play football in them.'

'Where do you play?'

'On the Heath. Sunday mornings. Beside the Lido. We get kids and all sorts.' He added, looking at me, 'Quite a few older blokes turn up.'

'Thanks,' I said. I was the one who made the jokes in my car.

As we went through Kentish Town he pointed to a large detached Georgian-style building at the bottom of the High Road which I'd never seen before.

'I'll be there tomorrow.'

'Oh yes,' I said. It looked like part of the Poly. Perhaps he was a college lecturer. A mad professor perhaps.

'Back to the dole,' he said.

'How terrible,' I said. 'It must be awful.'

'No, it's quite a laugh. The people behind the wires are the failures, not us. They get every spark of human kindness knocked out of them.'

He'd been on the dole since he left university, so he said. He'd had a few odd jobs, but hated them.

'I know the feeling,' I said.

'Do you?' he said, looking at me. Again, I wasn't sure if he was mocking me.

'Ok, I don't know the feeling. Which is your street?'

He'd turned my natural sympathetic reactions back on me. I was just being kind. I don't mind people being on the dole. If you've no responsibilities and you're young like him, what does it matter. He was quite happy with one pair of plimsolls. I rather admired him, sticking out against the rat race.

'I'll recognise it when I come to it,' he said as we cruised down Tufnell Park Road. 'Here we are.'

As we drew up, two beautiful children came running out of a block of flats to meet him. They had strange, odd clothes on, bare feet and incredibly blond hair like Midwich Cuckoos. Behind them came a woman carrying a baby, all smiles at the sight of Zak, the prodigal returned. He almost disappeared from sight as all four of them covered him in kisses and cuddles. He pulled himself away and came over to me very stiffly. 'Thanks. Great. See you.'

What a bastard, I thought as I drove away. A wife and three lovely kids and he's frigging off round Europe enjoying himself instead of getting himself a job. And with a degree. Bloody hell. I know the working man can have it hard when he's laid-off. But a graduate! They're crying out for teachers, aren't they. You meet some right shockers in this business. And he thought I was old. It had been even going through my head at one time to slip him a couple of quid for a new pair of shoes. Not now. I thought I was a selfish bugger. But bloody hell. Screw him.

3

I was taking the back-doubles way to London Airport to meet Joff. Having no sense of direction, it had taken me weeks to master it. The North Circular takes twice as long, if not more, when there's a jam, but Mr Innocent's secret way was so complicated that at first I had refused to try and master it. You can't do it from the map, because there are so many one-way streets which only he knew how to avoid. In the end, having got lost for four hours, I'd had to go with him in his car for six trips. I got to see the Master at work which of course was an experience no one should miss.

The dodgy bit is in Acton where if you miss the right side-turning you end up going down Western Avenue the wrong way with no means of getting off or across and you go on for ever and ever until you fall off the edge of the world. But having watched the Master at work, I knew that Victoria Road was the one you followed instead of carrying on straight down Wales Farm Road. That'll be five guineas.

I was on my own, which I shouldn't have been. Mr Innocent had things so well organised that you were never empty if possible, especially with the airport. You went there with someone as well as bringing someone back. But I didn't want some old woman chuntering on in the back seat about missing her plane while I tried to negotiate with the book on my knee.

I did it so well, without missing one turning, that I was at the airport half an hour early. I went for a drink. Joff's plane was half an hour late which meant by the time he arrived I'd had quite a few drinks.

It was the first airport I'd had for two weeks and I'd only got it because of Joff. No one would pick him up except me. Even Mr Innocent got out of it if he could. Joff always asked for me, though God knows why. I didn't particularly like him. I just told him to get stuffed every time he started. All the same, if I'd been the boss of the firm I wouldn't have had such an objectionable bloke in any of my cars. Mr Innocent maintained he was famous, with lots of contacts, and was very good for business.

He came through the gateway from Customs as if he'd just bought the place, tall and striking, with thick blond hair swept right across, incredibly good looking in an English public school sort of way. He had sun glasses on, trying hard to look as famous as Mr Innocent thought he was, and he was smiling into the air, knowing everyone was watching. The girls were all supposed to be panting for him but to me he looked one big phoney. He showed it in his work. He had no regard for anyone's feelings. Yet somehow in the end he always got away with it, because of his looks and because of his charm.

I wasn't going to rush forward and say Mr Jonathan Howard very loudly so that everyone could hear it was the real live Jonathan Howard. Mr Innocent, who could be a real creep at times, always had a large board with his name writ large on it, 'Jonathan Howard, BBC'. I stood at the back, waiting till he saw me. He knew me perfectly well. I'd decided to give him a few moments of worry and make him think we weren't there to meet him. Without me he'd be forced to get a taxi for himself and his minions, which would cost him a fortune and would have to be paid in cash. He treated us as if we were his private chauffeurs, exclusively at his beck and call. As I stood watching him, urging myself on to be myself and keep back, I felt myself going smaller and smaller. He did look Somebody.

'Joff,' I said as quietly as I could, moving forward, hating myself. I was losing my manhood just by the act of calling him by his nickname, creeping to him. I was as bad as Mr Innocent.

'Where the hell have you been?' he said, angrily. I couldn't think of a smart reply. I've changed a lot over the years, but there are still some people who have the power to browbeat me, just by their presence.

'Bloody well help them,' he went on, turning round, shouting at me over his shoulder. 'Don't just stand there.'

His p.a. and his researcher were struggling behind with his cases. They'd only been to Hamburg for three days but he travelled like Elizabeth Taylor with enough luggage for an army. Probably all full of whips and leather outfits. If it moved, Jonathan Howard laid it, male, female or animal. If all the old dears who watched his charm on the tele knew what he was like in real life, or, in his case, unreal life, they'd switch off for good. My Gran loved him and wouldn't believe my stories. She said I was just jealous.

I took a bag each from his p.a. and his researcher, both of whom couldn't speak but just nodded at me. They were loaded down with their own trendy gear, like rings and bracelets and leather coats. As we marched in procession downstairs he kept up a non-stop flow of oaths and complaints. I tried to keep quiet. I didn't have to take Joff or anyone. I didn't need them, or their money. I looked upon my dealings with Joff as a penance.

'Why weren't you inside?' he snarled.

'You mean Holloway? They've just let me out.'

'Don't try to be funny with me. I mean *inside* Customs, to help us get the bags through.'

'It's illegal.'

'Don't give me that. Innocent is always there. If he can do it, so can you.'

'He hasn't done it for four weeks.'

'What bloody lies. He was here when we came back from New York only two weeks ago. Caroline, when was New York?'

'Five months ago, Joff.'

'You're fired,' said Joff, throwing open the door of my car, not even waiting for the bags to be stowed away or for Caroline to get a seat. Caroline had a beautiful soul and agreed to everything from Joff, but with her awful figure she deserved the best seat every time. She was small and very squat with long tangled hair and

looked as if she might work on a fairground. Her incredibly posh
voice was always a big surprise.

'He got fined £20 for trespassing,' I said, sitting down beside
him when at last we were loaded up. 'He'd had this arm-band he'd
found years ago which said something like Olympiad. He used to
put it on and go straight through Customs as if he owned the airport. No one ever questioned him.'

'Incredible,' said Caroline, genuinely interested.

'Amazing,' said the researcher, equally enthralled.

'What the hell are you talking about?' said Joff, staring out of
the window, refusing to take any notice of me or my stories. He
turned the car radio up louder. I turned it down.

We drove in silence for a while. It had obviously not been a successful trip.

'Are you reporting this one?' I asked.

'I do everything,' said Joff. 'Otherwise how the fuck does anything ever get done.'

'How was it, then?' I said, turning round to Caroline and the
researcher, jammed tight in the back with half the luggage. Joff
had pushed his seat back even further than normal to give himself
more room. I wanted to chat to them not him. I hate swearing in
front of women.

'The research was useless,' said Joff. 'I had to do the programme
from scratch when I got there. And the hotel was the worst I've
ever stayed in.'

'On the Reeperbahn was it?'

Joff looked at me and turned away. No one else was allowed to
show any knowledge of anything, least of all a driver. But they're
all like this at the BBC and in the film world generally. They get
a little bit of technical mystique and it goes to their heads. They
think no one outside can understand their world, as if anyone
would want to. You can see for yourself whether a product is a
load of rubbish. Who cares how it's made.

'Did you go to the Eros Centre?' I asked, keeping up the chat,
though God knows why. 'I once knew a girl who worked there.
Lovely rooms, she said, but the only blokes who could afford the
big fees were Japanese with little wee-wees.'

Caroline and the researcher laughed. Joff didn't. He was the one who was vulgar or obscene. It wasn't like me, being vulgar. Joff was making me like him.

'When we get in I don't want you nicking off, you two. I want that stuff sent to rostrum and I want that Eclair checked. He's not taking that out again with me. And don't forget the 20.1 zoom for tomorrow.'

We drove through the gates at Shepherds Bush. He wouldn't let me stop, even though the barrier was down. They knew him and they'd better open it sharpish. It just got up in time, with the commissionaire saluting as soon as he saw him.

'You can stay here,' he said to me. 'I'll need you later to take me home.'

He'd already told me that the BBC would be paying, Caroline would look after that. As usual, he was extending the cab for his private use. He marched through the swing doors and was gone. As Caroline struggled with the luggage she told me not to sit in the car. Come to the canteen. She'd tell me when Joff was ready.

I went up in the lift with her and we went to the canteen. All Joff's unit were seated round one circular table, crammed so tightly they could hardly move their elbows. I recognised one or two faces from previous trips with Joff.

'He's not really like that,' said Caroline apologetically as we queued up.

'He's been like that every time I've met him.'

'We've had a terrible trip. If it hadn't been for him, the whole thing would have been scrapped. He is brilliant, really. That makes up for so much, don't you think.'

'No. It still doesn't excuse being nasty.'

'But he can be so kind. The thing is he's terribly insecure.'

'That's what they say about everyone who's nasty.'

As I said that, I almost dropped my tray of shepherd's pie. I'd heard a row at the front of the queue as I joined it. Now I saw the centre of it was Mr Innocent. He was arguing with the West Indian woman on the cash desk, maintaining she'd overcharged him. He was carrying a BBC folder and had his tie off and looked like some middle-aged arty-crafty producer, from somewhere in BBC 2. He

was reaming off the list of prices like a regular, and what they'd
been last week and the week before. I could see she'd given in and
was handing back some money. Mr Innocent went to the water
fountain and filled himself a glass. As he turned, he caught sight
of me. He was almost contorted, making so many faces, signalling
that I hadn't to recognise him. He walked past me, humming to
himself, making notes on his file. I could see on the till he'd got
away with a three-course meal for only 25 pence. It would have
cost him three times that outside.

'Don't I recognise that chap?' said Caroline.

'I was going to ask you that,' I said, 'I've seen his face but I can't
place it. Is it Cliff Michelmore?'

'No, he hasn't got as much hair as that. I think he's from
Horizon.'

Mr Innocent had a list of institutions around London which he
honoured with his presence every time he was in the area, either
parking in the directors' car park or having the cheap meals in
the canteen, usually the executive one. For every one, he had a
foolproof story about who he was and what authority he had to
be there. In our sort of job, you learn a little bit about important
people in many firms, so it's easy to think up alibis. Not that Mr
Innocent was ever asked.

I sat down with the unit, thanks to Caroline forcing me, though
I didn't want to. I'd been with them once before and they were
such a cliquish set who talked non-stop about Joff, what he'd said,
what he was doing, wearing, eating, sleeping, drinking, laying,
goo goo goo for hours on end about how awful he was but how
marvellous.

I looked round for Mr Innocent. I'd obviously spoiled it for him.
He'd probably gone with his vol-au-vent and glass of water into
the Director-General's suite, saying he was from McKinsey.

Caroline, whom I soon realised was everybody's dogsbody, not
just Joff's, was delegated to get the coffee. It took hours working
out who wanted cream and milk, hot or cold, getting in all the
money then dragging back, balancing all the cups. Why they
didn't all sit sensibly, four at a table, I didn't know. It was about
three o'clock and the canteen was almost empty. We were the

only people there, yet there they were, twelve to a table, jammed like sardines, each one scared to go and sit elsewhere and miss the latest Joff gossip.

I think Caroline enjoyed going for the coffees. She knew no one would go till she came back and they went through her stories about what Joff did in Hamburg for the second time round.

'Oh Franko, I've forgotten yours. How awful.'

'No no, it's ok. I didn't want one anyway.'

'Do you know, in the Grosse Freiheit,' said Caroline setting the coffees down, all breathless, 'Joff sent back his Schnapps three times because he said it wasn't the right temperature.'

'He didn't!'

'Honestly.'

'Fantastic.'

'Typical Joff.'

I had to leave. There was no room to be sick at the table. Caroline didn't notice me leaving, having captured the audience once more.

I sat in my car listening to Terry Wogan and his Fight on Flab for thirty minutes when at long last Caroline reappeared, bursting with apologies in her well-brought-up, BBC way.

'So sorry. I went to fetch you a coffee as well. You shouldn't have gone. The thing is, Joff now says can you wait just thirty more minutes. Will that be ok?'

I knew Joff's thirty minutes. That meant an hour. But as with all my dealings with Joff, I tried not to give away my feelings, to get beaten or made furious by him. What were my real feelings anyway? I hated him, so I kept telling myself. On his own, not performing to an audience, he wasn't so bad. At least I'd have him on my own on the way to his home.

'The thing is,' said Caroline again.

'Not another thing,' I said wearily. She giggled brightly.

'Sorry. Actually, his wife has arrived. I've never seen her before. She's super. And his son. Absolutely super as well. Must rush. Actually, I've been sent to get him a Coca-Cola.'

She padded away in her Biba boots. So Joff hadn't even remembered I was there. Only Caroline realised I'd be waiting. He expected his driver to wait for days, until he deigned to reappear.

I started the engine. It had happened again. I never knew he had a rotten wife. She could drive him. I was going home.

4

I parked at Gospel Oak beside the Lido and ran on to the Heath. Gran thought it was disgusting, a bloke of my age, going round the Heath asking kids if I could play with them. But how else could I get a game? And anyway, they weren't all kids. I never played with anyone under ten, unless I was really desperate.

It was lovely to be back. Now that I'd settled down in the job I'd worked out my own routine and took at least a couple of hours off every afternoon, despite what Mr Innocent said. I knew I was valuable to him, being a conscientious bloke, so I could afford to knock off when I'd had enough. I didn't need to make a huge wage after all.

As a kid I'd spent every afternoon on the Heath, straight from school to play football. I couldn't understand how for ten years I'd never kicked a ball. I'd never even thought about it. Now it had suddenly become the point of every day, to try to get a kick around before I went home. All I wanted was to get a sweat up, then go home, have a shower and feel cleansed. Oh such virtuousness. I suppose it was about time.

There were some Italian waiters, in very short shorts, practising high stepping and overhead kicks. I'd played with them before. They played most afternoons between meals. But they were just packing up as I arrived. They were going to finish off with a swim in the open-air pond – the Lido was still closed till the summer – but I refused. It had to be 80 degrees before I fancied an open-air swim, after what I'd become used to.

I met some Irish labourers, just coming off work, sitting on the grass, untying their trousers and hauling their filthy shirts over their heads till they were down to their vests and swimming costumes, all ready for action. It's always a rough game, playing with the Irish. They have little skill but they go in like tanks. I didn't want to be crippled. I wandered on, but I couldn't see anyone else, so I came back, waiting till they were ready. Their accents were so broad I couldn't understand what they were saying to each other. The Italians made more sense. Then one of them pointed to a shinty stick. They weren't going to play football after all. That was the last game I wanted to play. They hit each other like maniacs and the ball is like iron. Even when I see them playing miles away, I make a detour so I don't get hit with the ball.

The Heath has so many little communities, each with its meeting place, its own regulars, its own rituals. There's the kite flyers on Parliament Hill, all strange clothes and wild eyes, standing transfixed for hours, talking to each other by signs not words. The race-track runners, pounding round for hours then trudging away disappointed, with their little secret bags. The walkers, all arms and legs, going up and down like matchstick men, followed by kids shouting at them. The fishermen with their all-night vigils and green umbrellas. The middle Europeans at Kenwood with their camel hair and German accents, working out which seat to have dedicated to themselves when they die and have looked their last on all things lovely. The open-air swimmers, small and wiry and middle aged. The model yachtsmen with their complicated rules and flags and stop watches, turning a simple hobby into a secret society so that outsiders can't follow it.

At last I found a gang of kids beside the tennis courts, aimlessly kicking a plastic ball. I recognised one of them, a ginger-headed yob in big boots, and I asked him if I could join. He didn't say anything. I suggested picking sides, now that my arrival took their numbers from seven to eight. He didn't answer. I made another goal out of coats and moved them back. I knew I was going too far, moving in on their little knockabout. But it's always so much better to have a game rather than shooting in. They were all about fifteen, half my age. I was glad I hadn't put my shorts on. I would really have been out of it. They were in suit trousers, braces, Ben Sherman shirts and brown polished boots. I only hoped I didn't fall over and they'd see I had real football socks and boots on under my long trousers. They'd take me for a right fairy. I'd been kicked badly on the bone three weeks ago and had been forced to stop playing for a week. My life fell to pieces. The days had no point to them. Gran had been disgusted. A grown man, living for football.

Ginger was very good and I was glad I was on his side. His dribbling was excellent and the way he ran past people, holding and shielding the ball, was very professional. It was on the tip of my tongue to ask him if he played for anyone, but I knew better than to talk. I was an outsider. I didn't speak the language. Fifteen years ago, I'd been like them, rushing home from school, straight onto the Fields, and then when it got dark, back to the streets to hang around. Anything I said to them now would be condescending. I had to keep silent, keep my place and pass to Ginger when he shouted. He never stopped shouting, swearing and thumping any of our team who made a bad pass. Our goalie, who was a rush goalie, bringing the ball up the field, got beaten and they scored an easy goal. Ginger went up and kicked him, as he was lying on the ground. I can understand him kicking the opposition, but not our own side. I made sure I made no mistakes. I didn't want to incur Ginger's wrath. When we finished he said see you tomorrow. We play here every day at this time. I felt myself grow bigger. I was accepted. I'd been knighted. My days of soliciting might at last be over.

I went to get a paper on the way home, but found I'd no money. I'd deliberately kept three new pence in my trouser pocket, but it must have dropped out playing football. The paper boy had been at school with me. He let me off, telling me to pay tomorrow. It's nice being a local. They say London has no neighbourliness. You have to live there to know that it has.

I remember going to Finchley at fifteen for my first job and feeling I was in a foreign land. I spent all my time there trying to get out. It had been my Gran's fault, this idea that I wanted to be a hairdresser. The only thing I'd been good at at school had been art so, naturally, everyone wanted something artistic for me. Her friend was the cleaner at this Finchley salon and it was through this inside contact that I'd been dragged along and taken on as a junior. I schemed for two years to get a move up West but in the end I left. I hadn't learned very much and I didn't like any of the people. They were all so serious and back-biting. Funnily enough, when I went back to hairdressing, years later, I was so much better. I think it was with having knocked around a bit, got more confidence, that I was able to chat up customers and pretend I not only knew what I was going to do to them but that it was what they really wanted anyway.

I wondered what they were all doing, back in that Mayfair salon. I'd left in such a hurry I'd hardly said cheerio. I was sure Johnny hadn't left, though he was always just about to. I shared a flat with him for a while, which was murder. He turned out to be a sex maniac. He had continual rows at work and was always trying to get me to leave with him and set up in partnership on our own. We'd both signed contracts, saying we wouldn't open salons within a mile radius, but that didn't worry Johnny. The salon, and what I'd done afterwards, all now seemed light-years away, thank God.

I had a shower in my new lovely shower, an all-in-one affair that I'd seen advertised in a magazine. Gran said I was being daft. The bit of rubber hose over the bath was quite sufficient. I said it might be ok for her. I'd always known she was kinky. But I wanted a proper shower where I could stand up and enjoy myself.

The tatty bit of rubber in the bath was the only thing in the flat that was scruffy. All the rest of it was in very good condition. Not luxurious or opulent or showy. Just very good quality. I'd been surprised. From the outside, it had looked an ordinary red-brick anonymous Hampstead apartment block. The big advantage was that it was near my old Kentish Town stamping grounds. I hadn't bothered to notice that it was quite a posh neighbourhood.

I wasn't quite sure why I'd gone back to square one on such a big scale, what with the Heath, football and all the rest. Perhaps I was ashamed of having betrayed my roots.

I was ashamed of Johnny. I hadn't realised at first what had been going on. I'd struck up a friendship with him the first day I'd joined the salon. He had a spare room in his flat which was why I moved in with him. Almost every night he had blokes going in and out of his room. Then he'd started on me. It had just been a bit of horseplay, really. The usual sort of experimenting. One minute I'd go along with it, then the next I'd be consumed with guilt. It began to worry me. I knew I wasn't like that. It had never happened before. I didn't want it to happen again, which was one of the reasons I was back with Gran. Even though it was like going into cold storage, I felt much happier and safer.

After I'd had my shower, I cleaned it out and put everything tidy. I didn't want Gran moaning. I'd been trying to persuade her ever since we'd moved in that we should get a cleaning woman, just for an hour or so a day. As we were both working, it seemed silly not to. She said if I got a cleaning woman that was it, she was going.

I put on my pyjamas and dressing-gown, even though it was only seven o'clock. I was in for the night. It seemed a waste of time to get dressed only to get undressed again at ten o'clock. That was another part of my new, healthy, clean-living life. Early to bed, early to rise, not forgetting my ten minutes of Yoga every morning. Lord Baden Powell would be proud of me. A psychiatrist would have been very suspicious. What was I compensating for?

It was her late night, I forgot. I thought about putting the kettle on, but she likes to do everything by herself, though I knew she'd moan when she came in that I hadn't even put the kettle on. After fifteen minutes of thinking about it, I got up and put on the kettle. It boiled and she still hadn't appeared. I put the gas off. When I heard the lift gates going, I jumped up and put the gas on again, hoping she wouldn't notice. She did. The first thing she spotted was the steamed-up windows.

She was laden down with shopping bags, which was another thing she insisted on doing. I said we could get groceries delivered, but no. She'd always done it. She wasn't going to change her ways now.

I gave her a hug and took all the things off her and told her to sit down. I got her a Guinness and slowly she relaxed. I said there was no hurry, the meal could wait. I told her the details of my day, the latest on the awful Joff and on my other regular customers.

Then she told me about the shop, how each department was full of rumours that they were going to close. Some might get moved to another shop in the chain, but she was sure she wouldn't.

They'd pay her off. Forty years' service, but they didn't care.

Ever since I came to live with my Gran, as a little boy of two, she's been going to get paid-off. I'd ceased to worry, but I made the appropriate noises. Then she went over her day, chronologically, about who had said what and at what time and to whom. I loved all her work stories, and she loved all mine. I've never lived with anyone, male or female, who was so genuinely interested in all my daily thoughts and actions. I didn't tell her everything, but almost. It was one of the reasons I'd asked her to come and live with me again. I felt slightly that I had to, as I'm her only relation and she did bring me up, but she would never have forced herself upon me. She'd worried about giving up her council flat, that she'd never get it back, but I said she hadn't to worry, I would look after all that.

We had porridge to start with and then stovies, which is a sort of hot-pot dish. I'm not even sure how it's spelled, but Gran weaned me on it. I've had all that smoked salmon scene, and all that Mediterranean wine. I've been through it all. For a cold London night you can't beat porridge and stovies, made the way Gran makes them.

'That's the stuff to give the troops,' she said as we washed up together. It was the same phrase she'd used every evening of my childhood when I helped her to wash up, each time coming out with it as if it were a brilliantly original remark. Then we watched Come Dancing on television and had cocoa at ten o'clock and went to bed, each to our separate bedrooms, wishing each other fond farewells and pleasant dreams.

I couldn't let Mr Innocent find out that sort of thing, could I. He would have murdered me. I'd have been the laughing stock of the firm. I couldn't let him find out anything.

5

'I tried several times to get you,' said the voice. It sounded familiar but rather strained, as if he was putting on a disguised voice or trying to be posh and well spoken.

'Oh, I'm always available,' I said, trying desperately to put a name to the voice. I've been not-known enough times in my life to hate not knowing other people's names.

'With interest, I've worked out I owe you about two quid.'

'Lovely.'

'Will you do some private work for me?'

Mr Innocent was watching me, trying to listen at the same time as he was filling in his income tax forms. The biggest crime in his book was when a driver tried to hive off a bit of business, picked up through his firm, and keep it to himself. He'd just told Midge he was sacked, though of course as he owned the office he wasn't going. A local businessman that we did a lot of driving for had asked Midge to put on a uniform and drive him to various factories in his Rolls. Midge maintained that this was a purely private arrangement. He was driving the bloke's own car, using his petrol, acting as a part-time chauffeur. It was nothing to do with Mr Innocent or Fantastic. It had everything to do with Fantastic, said Mr Innocent. Midge would never have met the bloke if he hadn't been one of Fantastic's customers. It was the sort of row which would go on for months and never be resolved. Mr Innocent was of course dead jealous.

'Heh, that's Midge back,' I said, putting my hand over the telephone. Mr Innocent was out in the road like a flash.

'Of course, Shaggy,' I said, speaking into the phone again. 'Anything you want. Well, almost anything.'

'*Shuggy*,' he said, dropping his new London accent and going back to Gorbals. I'd completely forgotten he'd never paid me.

'How are you then? Speaking from Glasgow are you?'

'Watch it. I want you to pick me up at my digs on Saturday at one o'clock, and every second Saturday after that, until I tell you not to. I'll expect a big discount for a regular order. Ok?'

I hardly recognised him. He had a suede jacket on that must have cost all of £50, brown wet-look shoes with a big buckle and hair down to his shoulders, all in two months. He'd become the reserves' top scorer in just six games and had once been substitute for the first team. As he hadn't actually played for the first team, I'd never noticed his name, although I pretended like mad I'd heard all about his success.

'It's not all that much faster, you know,' he said, stretching himself, sitting up front beside me.

'You mean compared with the Tube?'

'No, English football. I'd been told it would be. It's just that *every* match is hard. There are no soft games. In Scotland there's a big difference between the good teams and the rest.'

I didn't believe he'd been looking for me to pay me the fare he owed me. What had happened was that he'd been going on the Tube to the ground and had now decided, being so famous, that he was above that, at least for match days. It didn't matter on training days, rolling up at the ground at ten and leaving about one o'clock when there was nobody around. But on Saturday lunch times the Tube trains were always full. After a few weeks, some fans had begun to recognise him, so he said.

'You know what it's like, autographs, telling you how the team should be run, who should be fired, why we got beat last week. They don't understand, do they. You can't discuss it with them. You just agree, know what I mean.'

He'd even picked up an East End interrogative. It was all very appealing and wafer thin, this new-found confidence. One setback and he'd scurry for cover inside himself. I think he was coming on particularly strong with me as I'd intimidated him so much at the station that first day. Now he realised I was a normal figure on the scene, for London. He also wanted to show off his clothes. Joe Pagan, despite being a Londoner and two years older, was one of those boring work horses with short hair and short thighs whom managers love. I think Joe wore his club blazer in bed.

'Take Six?' I said, pointing to Shug's jacket.

'No, Gay Lord.'

'Get a discount?' I asked. 'Pro footballers can, you know.'

'Really, I didn't know that.'

'Got an agent yet?'

'Do you think I should?'

'Bloody hell. Georgie Best had one when he was still dribbling in his cot.'

I suggested he should really get an agent, for the future if nothing else. He could ask some of the first-team stars who they had. I
was humouring him, keeping up his new image of himself.

'I can't really,' he said, slowly.

'Don't they speak to you?'

He looked at me, trying to decide whether to tell the truth.

'Well, sort of. But you don't speak to them first, know what I
mean. But they're good lads. It's a lovely club. The boss is smashing. But they're all married with big flash cars and they all rush
off home or to their little businesses straight after training. The
reserves sort of stick together. Even in training, we don't use the
same dressing room or showers till they've finished. Wasn't like
that in Scotland. But I'll be in the first team soon. Don't worry. See
you Wednesday for the Arsenal game, ok?'

Their reserves were playing Arsenal reserves in something
called the Combination League. He was going on as if it was the
Cup Final. I arrived early at his digs and sat trying not to listen to
Mrs Pagan as she went on maligning the club. Joe was sitting with
his leg in plaster. Almost on the day Shuggy arrived, Joe had got a
broken leg.

'And you'd better be home early tonight, my lad,' said Mrs
Pagan to Shuggy as he came down in a maxi leather coat. 'I'm not
telling any more lies to the club about you. One night out a week's
enough.'

'But when you've got a Wednesday game, it's like a Saturday,
isn't it. You've got to celebrate, haven't you.'

'They'll hammer you,' said Joe.

'Put a quid on it then.' Shuggy took a pound note from his wallet
and gave it to Mrs Pagan. 'Come on then, you tight devil. Where's
yours?'

'He's got blue eyes, this lad,' said Mrs Pagan. 'I knew it the
minute he arrived. My Joe has never had any breaks right from the
beginning. He's been with the club since thirteen, trained there
twice a week and joined the staff the day he left school. Five years
he's given them. They don't appreciate you. Hughie's only been
here a week and he gets special treatment from the beginning, just
because he's foreign.'

'Oh give over, Mam.'

'Just you wait. One of these days I'll sell my story to the papers about what goes on up there.'

In the car Shuggy said that what he wanted was a little pad of his own up West, where he could have a bit of fun, know what I mean. He and Joe got on fine. He was a good lad. But Mrs Pagan was getting on his twat.

'The club wouldn't allow it, though. She's a registered landlady. I've got to stay with her, or some other old cow. You don't know a place do you? That I could use for the odd night? She watches me like a bloody hawk. She goes through my pockets for French letters every night.'

'I'll think about it. I might know somebody who could help.'

'I'll pay well, you know. I've got the best contract in the reserves, but don't tell Joe.'

He scored three goals before half time, all solo efforts. In the second half he just stood around looking beautiful, but by that time the match was won. I had a good seat in the stand because he'd given me a free ticket, big deal. They give away almost all the tickets for reserve matches. Shug was hoping I was going to fix him up with something. He'd got into his head I was a man of the world. But which world?

I stood by Gospel Oak Lido trying to look as if I had a good reason for standing around Gospel Oak Lido on a cold wet Sunday morning. The barbed wire at the top of the red-brick walls made it look even more like Stalag 19. As a kid, I'd always hated it, even on the hottest summer day. All the tough lads would throw themselves into the freezing cold water and maintain it was marvellous, come on in, you pansy. So I'd edge in, all goose pimples, and get straight out again. Then they'd get hold of me afterwards in those prison-like open changing rooms and flick me with their towels and grab my balls as I tried to hide myself inside the cubicles which never lock, hoping one of the attendants would come and save me, but they never did. They'd all parade round, stark naked, while I watched, and have competitions. I can still remember them and what each boy looked like. I'd watch, but never take part, until one day I was forced to. At the time, I was very worried by my interest in watching them. That's probably what made all the difference.

Two coloured girls came past, arm in arm, giggling as they passed me, stalking off towards Parliament Hill. They were giants, both of them, all legs and huge thighs, wearing the smallest of school-girl skirts. They were bursting out of their clothes, everywhere, yet they could only have been about thirteen.

A park keeper walked round me three times, very suspicious. He had a beard on, which parkies never had when I was a kid, and was obviously out to be a senior keeper before the day was over. I'd already seen him chase a gang of kids playing football, moving them from the hockey pitch over to the rough stuff beside the One O'clock Club. He'd warned two girls for cycling and an old man for having a transistor. I felt like telling him I'd seen a greyhound without a cage-type muzzle, but I didn't want to draw attention to myself, more than my baggy tennis shorts, baseball boots and sun glasses were already doing.

That had been one of the phrases from my childhood, Greyhounds Must Wear Cage-type Muzzles. You don't see it in London Parks these days. Greyhounds went out when scampi and Ford Capris came in. I never knew what it meant. It was one of those phrases like Gladly my Cross Eyed Bear which children naturally get wrong because it's so big and cumbersome. The parkie came past me for the fourth time, smelling my Aramis, and this time I decided to move further away. Perhaps the meeting place had been changed from the Lido.

Then I noticed that one of the kids playing football beside the fence was not a kid. In fact, only four of them were kids. The other seven were blokes. There was a pair of blue-painted plimsolls I recognised.

'Hi,' I said, getting near Zak. He took a kick at the ball and fell over. He looked at me and didn't answer. Then he went pelting after a ten-year-old who'd taken the ball from beneath him. He obviously didn't recognise me. I shouldn't have put the white shorts on. That was my first mistake.

I thought it would be a proper match for a change, with goal posts, football strips and everything. I'd made an effort and put on my lovely white tennis shorts. I'd bought them years ago as part of the full gear when for half an hour I'd decided to take up tennis. Looking up towards the hill where the real players were playing, I realised that even amateurs had very short sexy shorts these days. At least I hadn't put my hair in a middle parting.

'Can I join in?'

Zak didn't answer. He was flying up the field, knocking the kids over. A bearded bloke in goal said I was kicking that way. I wasn't sure which way that way was or who was on whose side. I thought he pointed up so the next time Zak came down with the ball I took it off him, belted after it, beat two kids to round the goalie and score. Then I lay down on the grass, exhausted, my little heart beating. If I'd been playing with Ginger, I'd have been trampled on. I'd thought I was fit. It must be true that one run up the field equals three miles of sex.

'You bloody fool,' said Zak. 'You're on my side. They're winning now.'

I had about ten minutes on the ground, recovering. By that time I'd worked out who was on whose side. The little kids had the talent while the big lads had all the strength, so it was fairly even. I came somewhere in between, with more talent than the big lads but not as much strength. I'd always had a slight skill for ball games, but being so small and weedy as a child I always got knocked over. Now with all the practising I could be quite flashy, keeping it in the air, or overhead kicks, but not when it came to beating the big lads in the mud.

I think Zak was quite impressed, expecting me to be a real Jessie. Nobody else was any good so I kept up my end quite well. Playing against kids helped. I could take them on and knock them over, even some of the bigger lads. Being an adult, or at least passing for an adult, I had more confidence than I had as a child, which is a major part of strength. I went in knowing I could do it. I can understand it now when managers say that when a player has developed as a personality he'll develop as a footballer. They go together, as had obviously happened with Shuggy. He'd found his feet, on and off the pitch.

There was a lot of arguing. Their biggest lad was an Irish navvy, by the sound of his language, who was furious when anyone didn't do what he told them. The heavy on our side was an Ulsterman who was equally raucous. They were always on different sides, so I gathered. When they played on the same side it was worse because they blamed each other and usually came to blows. I was told later that both of them were lecturers at the London School of Economics.

We all got changed on the side afterwards. I'd brought my long trousers and a pullover to put on over my tennis shorts. My Gran says you should always cover up after you get hot. She also says that the best drink when you're sweating is hot sweet tea. The *Sunday Post* advice column has a lot to answer for.

Zak was much better built than I'd expected. He stripped right down to his underpants, giving us all the benefit of his muscles. The two LSE blokes even had track suits. Very professional.

'What you looking at?' said Zak. I blushed instantly. I'd only glanced at him for a second and I was sure he hadn't noticed.

'You're not my type,' I said, quickly, but not very convincingly.

'Too butch, eh,' said Zak. 'Hand us me skirt then, don't just stand there like a spare prick.' I turned to where he was pointing and they all laughed. I honestly thought he'd said shirt. Luckily, one of the others started talking about the Spurs match the previous day and they soon forgot me. Zak was in the thick of it, arguing just for the sake of arguing, contradicting everyone's opinion, telling them they were idiots yet without annoying them. When the two LSE heavies waded in it became like a tutorial, despite their funny Irish accents, and everyone made faces. Zak's was Northern, but I couldn't tell which part. North of Watford they all talk alike to me. Except Scottish. I could tell Shuggy's accent straight away.

Still arguing, as if he'd forgotten me, Zak started walking away with the others. Then over his shoulder he said come to the pub, knowing I would follow. He was wearing exactly the same jeans, T shirt and plimsolls he'd played football in. I couldn't understand what all the changing had been for.

I bought the first round, which was probably a bit flash, but as the stranger and a working man, I thought I should do the right thing. Being basically mean, I have to get in first, just to show I'm not mean, then I'm in contortions watching to see who doesn't buy his round.

The conversation was still about yesterday's League results. The two LSE blokes hadn't come. Their wives wouldn't let them, so they said. I would have preferred to have gone home and had a shower first. Gran says never let a sweat dry on you. But having found a new gang to play football with, much better and more organised than Ginger's gang or any of the week-day knockabouts, I wanted to keep in with them. That's what I told myself anyway. I could still feel my ears red from Zak's joke, though everyone else had forgotten it.

Zak got up and moved to the bar. I wanted to stop him, to tell him I didn't want another drink. The others still had the pint I'd bought them. Zak was being daft. He was making the gesture, just to show being on the dole didn't matter.

I'd been thinking about him a lot since we'd first met. My first reaction had been that he must be a sod to stay on the dole when he had so many responsibilities. But it was having so many responsibilities which made his stand all the more valid. A single bloke like me could go on the dole because nobody else would be affected. There were no pressures on me to conform. But Zak had everything against him. Yet he stuck to his principles. I didn't know if I would stick to mine, if I knew what my principles were.

He was standing quietly at the bar, waiting his turn, casual and cocky. I suppose I was beginning to like him. He opened up a plastic lid on the food counter and carefully chose four pies and put them on a plate. He was overdoing it now. I wasn't even hungry. The others had already had crisps and hadn't offered Zak any.

The queue was slow-moving, with the usual loud Sunday morning pre-lunch hearties, all in their best check shirts and neckerchiefs, shouting out their phoney fascist chat to the landlord. Zak got fed up and went to the lavatory, carrying his plate of pies. When he came out again, he was empty-handed. There was no sign of the plate or the pies.

He sat down beside me and joined in the conversation about Arsenal's chances in Europe. I tried to catch his eye, to look at him, but he had his usual conversational smile, even when he was telling them all they were stupid and that they knew as much about football as the football writers, and they were all cretins. Then he got up and said see you next week.

He took it for granted that I should walk home with him. He didn't even ask where I was going or whether I lived near by or whatever. We walked for a long time in silence. I was trying to work out what I was doing.

'How's the dole?' I said at length.

'The same. It can't change can it.'

'I read that the Government's going to have a new enquiry.'

'They don't care.'

'That can't be true. It's bad publicity, having a million out of work.'

'That's what the Tory Government wants. It's old Keynesian philosophy. They don't mind an unemployed sector, but they don't want that sector to have no spending power. So they give them dole money to enable them to buy things. That's the main reason for dole money.'

'I can't believe it.'

Zak looked at me. In his own little world, on the dole, out of work or not, he obviously wasn't used to being contradicted. He had a way of staring at you and then suddenly smiling and looking away. It was when he looked away that he said things which came over indistinct and blurred, and if you weren't concentrating or waiting for him to speak you missed it.

'I was absent when they did history,' I said.

'I wished I'd left at fifteen,' he said. 'I got on a conveyor belt and I couldn't get off. At eleven they said, quick, French or German. Then at thirteen it was quick, Science or Arts. At eighteen, it was quick, Training College or University. I woke up at twenty-one finding myself doing a degree in engineering when I wasn't the slightest bit interested in university or engineering or a degree. I'd been brain-washed.'

'What do you want to do?'

He didn't answer. I might not have been there. It had all been a monologue. He'd turned and was climbing the stairs of his block, all in mid-sentence, without saying cheerio. I ran to catch up.

'Can I have a word with you?'

We were walking along an outside landing, about five floors up, all grey and solid stone and chalk marks on the wall.

'Go ahead,' he said, stopping and looking at me.

'Well, perhaps not here . . .'

He turned again and I followed him up one more flight and through a hand-painted door, a psychedelic explosion which had been done with a spray gun.

'Very phallic,' I said, admiring it.

Inside, the little flat was immaculate, with clean straw matting on the floor, lots of books neatly arranged and kids' paintings on the wall for decoration. His wife came out of another room, her breasts bare, the baby in one hand. I turned my head the other way.

'Sorry,' I said. 'If I'm disturbing you, I'll see you next week.'

'Don't be silly,' she said. 'Sit down. I'll just put the kettle on. We're always late with everything on a Sunday. Have you got the pies?' Zak took them out of his pocket and handed them to her.

'What a nice flat,' I said, looking round.

'It's grotty,' she said. 'But you should have seen some of the places we've lived in.'

'Same here,' I said. 'I once lived in a condemned house in the East End with a tramp who ate rats. He killed them by biting their heads off.'

'What did it look like?' said a voice behind me. A four-year-old boy, one of the blond bombshells, was watching me.

'It looked like a rat without his head on,' said his mother. 'Now go and get Tom. Your dinner's nearly ready.'

She went into the kitchen, brought me a mug of coffee and started to prepare the meal. I couldn't possibly accept, even if I was invited. They were obviously so poor. But she probably would ask. She seemed that kind of person. What she had was shared with whoever was there.

'We're trying to get a Co-op going at work,' I said to Zak. 'We have this boss at the moment, but the fuzz are after him for income tax fiddles and the rest. He's trying to sell the firm, not that anyone would buy it. We're trying to take it over, all the drivers, for a nominal sum. We'll all be equal partners and directors with no one more important than the other. It probably won't come off.'

I was talking quickly, thinking it was the sort of socialistic idea Zak might be interested in. I stopped and Zak stared at me, as if wondering who I was and how I'd got into his life.

'But you know what it's like,' I continued feebly, 'people get keen for a few days, then they go off it. They can't be bothered.'

'But you must,' said his wife. Zak groaned and she went back into the kitchen.

The Co-op had actually been Midge's idea, after they'd come to take Mr Innocent down to the police station for questioning. I'm all for good ideas, and helping people and all that and my heart's in the right place, so I keep telling myself, but it hasn't got to be too inconvenient, and I haven't got to do all the work.

'Can you drive?' I asked.

'No,' said Zak.

'I can,' said his wife, from the kitchen. 'Would you like me to join you?'

'It could fit in well with being a housewife,' I said. 'You need just do evenings. Zak could baby sit.'

I was getting keen again. His wife was all smiles.

'No,' he said severely. 'It's *my* job to get work, not hers. I'm the failure round here, remember.'

'We'll have to do something,' she said, going back to the kitchen. They'd obviously been through it all before, many a time. I looked at Zak's plimsolls. Those LSE heavies had been tackling too hard, or perhaps it had been me. Both his soles were coming away.

'What I was really going to say,' I started, shifting uneasily in my chair. 'I have this friend who has a girl but he lives in these terrible digs with a terrible landlady who won't let him do anything. Know what I mean? He's got bags of money. Well, he's looking for a room for a few hours now and again, you know, a bedroom.'

'So,' said Zak accusingly.

'Well, I was thinking. To help him out, and help yourself out. The dole people wouldn't know. No tax. When the kids are at school, say. Not even a bed, perhaps just a floor. You'd do it for a friend, wouldn't you . . .'

'Never,' said his wife, coming from the kitchen.

'It was only a suggestion,' I said, rising quickly. 'You need the money, don't you? What's the point of being all high and mighty . . .'

I was going to add, being on the dole, but I'd already regretted saying as much as I had done.

She stood glowering at me, waiting for me to leave, with Zak beside her. He was a big strong lad, as I'd already noticed in the park.

'I'm not turning this place into a brothel for whatever money,' she said. 'It's bad enough as it is.'

'Sorry I spoke,' I said. I got to the door and then turned, shouting to Zak. 'Thanks for the coffee.'

Zak came out of the kitchen to the door to see me out onto the landing.

'What's his name?' he said to me. 'Ask him to call round some time. She's always like that at first.'

I got a call from Caroline at the office, asking for me specially. She's a nice girl, but I'd never heard her so nice and pleading and worried. Could I go and fetch Joff? He was at home, very depressed over something. He had an urgent meeting with the Comptroller in the afternoon and if he didn't make it, he'd be for it. He'd not turned up the week before, without an excuse. The BBC didn't like that sort of thing.

'I just can't knock at the door and tell him to go to work.'

'You can, you can. He likes you.'

'What lies!'

'No, really. We've all tried and failed.'

'But it's nothing to do with me. He'll just say get stuffed.'

'He'll lose his job if he doesn't come.'

'That's his problem.'

'It's everybody's problem. He needs help. You live near him. You often bring him to work. Just arrive and say I've rung up, ordering a mini-cab for him. You don't have to know all the background.'

'No.'

'Ok. So I'm ringing up now, from the BBC, ordering a cab to

bring a Mr Howard to work. You can't refuse that.'

'I'm busy. It'll probably be Mr Innocent.'

I hung up. These bastards always seem to attract nice people round them. Everyone loves a rat. Joff was one of the biggest. He'd been boasting to me the previous week when I was taking him to Lime Grove that yes, he was a member of *the* Howard family, 'Duke of Norfolk and all that. Not absolutely direct of course, but pretty close. Christmas cards and all that shit.'

I'd believed it, till I had another BBC director in the cab who practically stopped at the first dry-cleaning shop to strip off when he heard he'd been sitting in the same seat as the awful Howard. He told me Joff's real name was neither Jonathan nor Howard. No one knew what his real Christian name was. Making up that soppy abbreviation was all part of his phoneyness. But someone once knew him at fifteen on a local paper in Slough and he'd definitely been called Bates in those days. When he got married he'd changed it to Howard to stop people calling him Master Bates. He maintained it was his wife's idea, who was even more of a snob than he was.

I went to the caff and had some tea. I'd keep Mr Bloody Howard waiting, whether he wanted me to come or not. I went into their lav, which we from the office all used, and had a wash and brush up. I wished I'd brought my toothpaste. I was sure my breath was smelling. And I hadn't washed my hair last night the way I'd intended to.

Joff had this bijou little Georgian house in a bijou little square in Hampstead, at the back of Heath Street. It was so narrow that if you stood at the front with your arms out you could touch both sides of the house. But it was Hampstead and it was Georgian.

I'd never stood on his step before, with my arms out or otherwise. He wouldn't allow cabs into the square as it was so small. We had to stay at the entrance and peep, once, and then wait. I drove right to his door and parked, blocking the whole square for everyone else. To hell with them.

I rang the bell and waited. Perhaps his wife was a snob, and worse than him and she'd soon chase me for daring to park outside their house. The door was opened by a tall tanned creature in tight trousers with one of those open-necked T shirts that has a cord which you tie across the top.

'Hello,' he said.

'I'm from Fantastic. Caroline sent me.'

'Of course. Come in.'

I entered along a hall which was almost as narrow as our office. It was all white with a deep pile carpet, a heavy white wallpaper and a mirror along the ceiling to make it look bigger.

'It sounds like a code. I'm from Fantastic. Caroline sent me. Where should I put the microfilm?'

The creature stopped and smiled, one hand opening a door to let me into the drawing room. 'Yes, doesn't it. Very KGB. I'm Eddie. After you.'

Joff was spread out on the couch, a glass in his hand, his jaw jutting out the way it always did when he was pretending to be really nasty to some pathetic politician.

'Who asked you to come?' he snarled.

'The KGB,' I said. 'They know everything.'

'Yes, the game's up, Joff,' said Eddie. 'You'd better go quietly.'

'You two think you're so bloody clever.'

'Well I am,' said Eddie. 'I don't know about your friend.'

Joff got up and went to the wall and kicked it. I could see a row of marks on the William Morris paper where he'd done it many times before.

'Why don't you just go back to bed,' he said to Eddie, 'which is where you belong.'

The creature didn't say anything this time. He was flickering his eyelashes at me. I liked his whole style, it was a bit like me only I was the B picture version. It was impossible to tell where the camp ended and the camp began.

'Have a drink,' said Joff to me.

'Not when I'm driving.'

'You're not driving. You're sitting in my house, for Christ's sake.'

'Her house,' said Eddie.

'I told you to shut up! I'm not going to the Beeb today. I made that perfectly clear to that half-wit. I'm indisposed.'

'Then I'd better go,' I said quietly.

'No don't, please sit down,' said Eddie, moving me to a seat, gently and softly. Perhaps I could become a bastard if I tried hard. If Joff got the sack from the BBC perhaps he could open a finishing school for them and I'd be his first pupil.

'Joff. You've got to go. There's no use mucking up the BBC. Whatever happens, you've got to keep your job.'

'I don't care.'

They looked at each other, cold and resigned. They'd been through it all before. The jokes were over.

'What's happened?' I asked, not expecting to be told.

'His wife's suing,' said Eddie, 'and I'm being cited as co-respondent.'

'You just have to deny it, don't you?'

'She's got proof,' said Joff, putting on his best agonised look. The bitch got hold of some letters I'd written. She employed some cunt to come into this house and steal them.'

'Sue them for breaking and entering.'

'What good would that do?' said Eddie. 'They've got the letters.'

'They were signed, by me,' said Joff, wearily. 'Written to Eddie. On BBC notepaper.'

I wanted to laugh but was scared in case Joff threw something at me. Somehow I wasn't scared at having the information, about being told something which later they might regret telling me. Joff told most people everything about himself. The problem was usually to work out how much he was exaggerating. This time I felt it was true and that they didn't mind telling me because they felt I'd understand and be sympathetic. So I couldn't possibly laugh. Eddie smiled at me, not laughing at Joff, just showing how much we both cared. Joff took it the wrong way and glared at us, as if we were both against him. Then he collapsed. He couldn't gather enough strength together to be furious.

Eddie clapped his hands, loudly, to wake him up and bring him back to his senses. He told him quickly and bad-temperedly that he was just being stupid and dramatising everything, as usual. It wasn't helping anything. It wasn't the end of the world. He should get ready and go with me, at once.

'What's the point?' said Joff. 'When it all comes out, I'll get the push anyway.'

'Christ, you deserve to,' shouted Eddie.

I wasn't sure if Eddie had lost all sympathy this time. Joff had crumpled away. He looked small and rather old. It was his confidence which made him seem powerful.

'Look, for the sake of the unit, you've got to go. Nothing need come out. And don't forget Toby. You're not helping him.'

The telephone rang. Joff wearily stretched out a hand to answer it. Eddie watched him carefully.

'Ok, ok, I'm coming. Don't nag me.'

He got up, put his jacket and tie on and pushed back his hair in the mirror while Eddie and I watched him. Then he turned to Eddie, put both his arms round him. They stood together, silently, Joff's head on Eddie's shoulder. I went to the door and waited outside in the car.

'You know,' said Joff, sitting beside me as we reversed out of the square, 'if anything happened to Eddie I'd probably commit suicide.'

6

About a month later I was standing in the car park at Spurs. It was like the back door at the London Palladium. You could hardly get moving for camel-hair coats, sun glasses and suede jackets. Getting into it had been like getting into Fort Knox, even though Shuggy had given me the right ticket. His team coach had just arrived and I'd lost him in a sea of hangers-on. Although they were only a second-division team, compared with the mighty Spurs, they were getting all the attention. It was the sixth round of the FA Cup and Shuggy's team had knocked out three first-division clubs already, with Shuggy scoring the winning goal each time. He was the new boy wonder. The evening papers had gone mad over him. The *Sunday Times* colour supplement had had a picture of him naked, naturally, doing his body exercises, showing all the dumb bells and exercises he used to build up his weight. The *Observer* was going to have him naked, naturally, this time stripped down in the dressing room afterwards, showing his black and blue body, the swellings on the ankle, the cuts on the knee, the gashes on his groin and the bruises on his thigh. Dennis Law wouldn't have a chance after that appeared. It would be on every bedroom wall, from Bayswater to Tangiers.

Shuggy disengaged himself from the throng, but only got three yards before a hand-held ITV team had him in a corner, asking him how he felt, was he nervous, what he'd had for breakfast, was he really engaged to Shirley Bassey or was that just a P. R. story. 'Utter rubbish,' he said, smiling his lop-sided smile. 'Anyway, I prefer Tom Jones.'

He got away, for three yards, then the press got him.

Had he heard that Leeds had offered £100,000 for him? No, he'd heard nothing at all. 'You shouldn't believe what you write in the newspapers.' They all collapsed, ho ho ho. What a wit, and only eighteen.

He managed another few yards, heading towards the ticket office, clutching a brown envelope. Shuggy might have become London's latest answer to Georgie Best in only three months and pestered for his views on everything, from pornography to Vietnam, but you could tell from the writing on the envelope that in many ways he was still only ten. It had obviously been done with great difficulty, sprawling in a spider trail across the envelope, starting big and finishing small, with some letters on the line below. Not that you expect footballers to be able to write, or talk, or read, or listen. From the age of ten, they've known that they were going to become professional footballers and that part of their being has been hyperdeveloped, as if under a glasshouse, while the rest of them has been completely ignored.

This was where Shuggy gained so much. Apart from being the new sensation on the field, and wearing all the right clothes, he had another plus which no footballer had been credited with before. He made jokes. They weren't brilliant jokes. They hardly stood repeating. But in context, they were said to be amusing, at least all the press fell about, just the way they fall about when that other brilliant wit, Prince Philip, sounds off to a gathering of the faithful.

'What has made you such a good footballer in so short a time, Shuggy?'

'I've got a good agent.'

That was another thing the press, especially the football press, loved. Unlike every other footballer, getting his Footballer of the Month award, he never thanked the team and his trainer and the coach and the man on the turnstile for being such lovely human beings. All the time, Shuggy made jokes at their expense, even that most sacred cow of all, the manager. He pretended he never did any training, cultivated the image of always being with at least two girls, made faces behind his manager when he was being interviewed after the Big Match. Yet the press still managed to give the impression that, of course, despite everything, Shuggy did work very hard and trained like a devil. I didn't actually believe it, not on what I'd seen of his private life. He was just lucky to be the only star in a second-division club. He could do almost as he liked because the gates had doubled, all because of him. A top first-division club would soon have knocked him into line.

I was still trying to examine the scrawl on the envelope, thinking how even that could be blown up across a double-page spread, when I noticed a camel hair, honing in on him. In a flash, the envelope was in his pocket and he was away, out of the car park and into the crowds on the High Road. For his four free tickets, Shuggy could probably make £50, even with the tout's percentage taken off. He must be making a bomb from his milk adverts and opening boutiques, but like most footballers, he couldn't make enough money. They have a short life, so Shuggy always told me, and they've got to make it while they can, in any way they can. Anyway, he personally wasn't making all that much, not yet anyway. It was just the press who said he was. He was in conflict with the club over his contract. It had seemed pretty big when he'd first arrived, compared with people like Joe Pagan, but after three months of making the club famous he didn't see why he should still be on the same basic terms, even though the contract had two years to run. Legally, the club had him. But logically, they wanted to keep him happy. They wanted everyone to be happy, as long as they were playing as well as Shuggy Gallacher was playing. Once Shuggy went off form, as was bound to happen, I didn't fancy his chances. The camel hairs would then suddenly become very thin on the ground. Shuggy of course just laughed at the very idea.

He scored one very lucky goal in the first five minutes, and after that he wasn't in it. He did about five solo runs, each time ending up where he'd started. He became hysterical every time he was robbed of the ball, claiming he was fouled, writhing on the ground in agony, arguing with the ref. Towards the end he kicked the ball into the crowd after a free kick went the other way and the referee took his name. While he was still sulking, Spurs scored and it was a draw.

All the same, he was still a hero in the next day's reports in the popular Sundays. He'd been built up so quickly by the journalists that they couldn't flatten him, not before they'd milked all the permutations out of him. There was that row with his club still to come, his architect-designed house in North Hendon, his first pop single. Most papers had agreed to buy exclusive rights to one or other of the goodies from an awful agent called Sammy who'd appeared on the scene and told Shuggy he would make him world famous.

'Shuggy does it again! He scored the goal which gave Hendon a draw and the right to meet the mighty Spurs again, this time at home. Despite ferocious tackling and some lamentable decisions by the referee, Shuggy's genius sparkled throughout the match. But will he be fit for Wednesday? That is the question all London will be asking this week-end.' It wasn't mine.

Joff was my first job Monday morning. I had to take him to Kensington House, one of the BBC's other buildings near Shepherds Bush. I hadn't been there before and I was worried I'd get lost in all the one-way streets off Holland Park. Joff was very reasonable and didn't get furious. He must want something. He said he'd direct me. Head first of all for the North Circular.

To make conversation, I asked how Eddie was. I'd heard he'd been ill.

'Still in hospital,' said Joff. 'He started to haemorrhage again. I don't think he's got polyps at all. Sounds more like an ulcer. That's what I had last year. Bloody painful. They gave me this bloody mediaeval instrument, like something out of a torture chamber. A dilator it was called. I had to use it every time I went to the bog. Bloody disgusting. It comes in three sizes. I had the biggest, of course.'

'Of course.'

'They say women have a rotten time with their troubles, but we can have it just as bad.'

'You did say the North Circular,' I said, regretting I'd started the conversation. I hated all Joff's personal confessions which he would go in for. In my little life, I've always steered clear of his sort of situation, both the physical and the mental. There are ways of doing it without all that mess. And as for all the bitchery and hysterics and rows and scenes and for ever changing partners and suspecting each other, there's no need for all that emotional stuff.

We drove left out of Golders Green Road and into the North Circular. I hoped Mr Innocent didn't see me. We weren't meant to use it. Every destination in London had his special back-double route worked out. All drivers were supposed to use them. That way we saved time, took more passengers and made more money for Mr Innocent.

As I was nearing fifty I passed a familiar figure, thumbing like mad on the pavement. I braked immediately, without quite knowing who it was, but knowing it was a friend. I reversed towards him, causing all the drivers behind to hoot and scream at me. At one time I would never have dared do such a thing with Joff as a passenger. But now that I knew so much about him, I had no compunction about doing a friend a favour.

'Get in,' I said, leaning over and opening the back door. Joff, now that we were friends, always sat in front with me.

'You're looking smart. Where you off to?'

'Oxford,' said Zak.

He had a new pair of shoes on, a three-piece suit, a shirt with a long collar and a kipper tie. He'd been pouring aftershave over himself as well.

'I've got an interview.'

'What for?'

'In a tech college. It's not my idea. It's all Sally's. But it's better than teaching in a school.'

Joff turned round and gave Zak his big famous smile, hoping to be recognised and asked for his autograph at least. As Zak didn't have a tele, I knew Joff would be out of luck. I also knew that in that case, Joff would expect me, as his latest acolyte, to introduce him, with his full name and pedigree and then lead the rounds of applause.

When the unit was out on location, it was part of Caroline's job to round up the peasants, whisper in their ear that it was Jonathan Howard, really, THE Jonathan Howard, from the BBC in London, England. There was always a handful of people daft enough to ask for his autograph. Joff was always beautifully surprised and charmed them all, without having the slightest suspicion that it had been a put-up job. He never questioned that he might not have been heard of. I saw it all happening once when I had to hang around a golf course at Potters Bar, waiting for him. I asked Caroline afterwards why she catered for his vanity, making him worse than he was. She said it was like a tonic for him. It bucked him up, made him work better and made him nicer to everybody. It also became a unit game, each one vying with the other to round up the locals.

Zak ignored Joff in the same way he'd taken little notice of me during that first meeting. Zak went according to waves. If they weren't immediately right and he decided you were sympatico, then that was it. You could try hard, forcing yourself upon him as I had done and gradually get his confidence, but if he didn't like the first vibration, then that was it. He certainly wasn't going to help. For someone like Joff, it became a challenge to impress himself on such people.

'I used to teach once,' Joff said, stretching himself. He'd got this TV habit of fitting an action, any action, to words and therefore you had double the chance of fixing people's attention. 'At my old public school. Eton wanted me to come for a Half, to help them out, but I told them to stick it. I got out soon afterwards and got into this crazy game.' Pause. 'The one I'm in now.'

Joff was cueing me like mad. I was grateful that Caroline wasn't there. She'd have been giving out Joff's curriculum vitae, the glossy hand-out version, before Zak had sat down in the back seat. Caroline was very efficient when it came to creating the Joff atmosphere. She was well aware of what she was doing. She wasn't as dumb as I'd suspected. In fact she was really ridiculing him a lot of the time. But she looked so naive and innocent, with her big gooey eyes and her Dilly Dream mannerisms, that it was hard to take her seriously. I could tell Joff was missing her. I was determined to keep him in his place.

I had a long and involved boring chat with Zak about the problems of getting a job when you were unemployed, saying how I'd been through the same thing a few years ago. The longer you were out of work, the harder it was to get work. Joff tried to get in on the act several times, but I ignored his interruptions.

Zak said he didn't want to have to give in and get the draggy, safe job which he could easily get, although he knew Sally wanted him to. I told him that ninety per cent of the country had draggy jobs and hated them. He'd stuck out so long. He shouldn't give in now.

'I'm preparing a programme on unemployment,' said Joff, all excited, having just thought of the idea. 'I think you could be just the person I'm looking for. What time have you got to be in Oxford? We'll pay your train fare. Can I talk to you for half an hour?'

Joff had at last got in. With one hand he was directing me round Shepherds Bush and with the other he was doing his performance about his nation-wide, earth-shattering programme.

'I can promise you,' he said, leering at Zak, 'it'll be an experience.'

They both got out, deep in conversation, without even closing the door. Zak was all animation, almost as if he'd been deliberately ignoring Joff in the car to make him keener. Joff had his arm round him, escorting him into the reception hall, acknowledging the nods of girls on the desk. It was as if Zak was going into a trap, with his eyes wide open. Joff was about to eat him up, like the very media he represented, corrupt and despoil him, bring out the worst in him, play to his baser motives. And I'd brought them together.

7

I met Eddie by chance on the Heath about a week later. I had about half an hour to put in before I was due in Bucks to pick up Shuggy from training. I decided to have a walk rather than discuss with Sparkle whether she should shave her legs every day or not. She was now sure it was her legs which were going to make her, so of course she had to be ready.

He looked so much taller than he'd done inside Joff's house. Perhaps it was being ill that had done it. I said so to him, not really meaning to. It was such a daft remark. He probably didn't want people mentioning his illness. I would have kept it very quiet.

'I *feel* taller,' he said smiling. 'You wouldn't believe how small I was in hospital.'

'I feel big when I'm driving the car,' I said. 'You wouldn't believe how small I am when I take it off at night.'

'Well, it's nice to know how we both feel.'

We walked for a bit, saying nothing. We'd both blurted out the idiot remarks, surprising ourselves. As he didn't seem embarrassed about having been in hospital, I asked him if he was better now. He said he was. It had all cleared up. It meant separate beds for a while, but that was just as well as his mother was coming for the weekend.

'Has she been before?' I asked, really meaning, does she know about you and Joff.

'No,' he said, answering what he knew I'd asked. 'I'll have to pretend we're just good friends. She'd be so hurt if she knew.'

Eddie obviously wasn't hurt. It was all perfectly natural. He seemed to have no hang-ups. He said that Joff would have to do some of the cooking and cleaning for a change, which would be a laugh, just to prove to his Mum that the housework was shared equally.

He asked me where I lived. I told him about my Gran and how she did everything. I was useless in the house. He was genuinely interested and asked me all about her. People like Zak and Shuggy

and even Joff never asked me anything about myself. I was interested in them, but they weren't interested in me, not that I minded,
really. It was nice to observe for a change. I was about to ask Eddie
how he'd met Joff when a plastic football came rolling towards me.
I ran to kick it and saw that it was Ginger who was playing. He had
his mate with him, a thug called Vince with cross eyes that I didn't
like the look of.

'Playing Sunday, then, Ginge?' I shouted, showing off, though
there wasn't much to boast about in knowing Ginger. Perhaps I
was letting Eddie see that I wasn't like him. We stood watching
them kicking the ball to each other, both with big heavy boots and
dark Crombie overcoats. They looked ridiculous.

'He's a good player, old Ginger,' I said. 'You should see him
stripped off on Sundays with our team.' Eddie smiled. I hadn't
meant it like that, but I pretended I did.

'Wanna game?' said Ginger, picking the ball up. I could see him
looking Eddie up and down.

'No thanks,' I said, 'I'm working.'

'Fuck off then,' said Ginger, turning away and kicking the ball
viciously towards Vince, who was lying on the ground scratching
his balls.

I walked round one of the ponds with Eddie and then said I had
to get back to work. Ginger had spoiled everything. We'd been
having a good chat, but now I felt embarrassed and self-conscious,
worried almost at having had such a good chat.

I decided to go up the M1 to Bucks, though I hadn't gone that way
before. The previous time I'd been there I'd been given directions
from Hendon. I was due at 1.30, which was when they finished, but
it could go on longer if they'd had a bad morning. I hoped they'd
had a bad morning. I wanted to watch them.

I drove up the cinder track and parked beside the sports cars.
There were two training pitches, one where the first team was
training and one for the reserves. Each team was practising dead
ball situations, like free kicks and throw-ins.

Then the reserves came from their session and together they
had a full-scale training game, the first team against the reserves.

It was far rougher than any match I'd ever seen Shug play in on a Saturday afternoon. The reserves were out to get the first team, especially Shug. They had their heads down and went into every tackle like tanks. They raced back furiously when beaten and if a colleague made a mistake, the shouts and arguments could be heard for miles. At a proper match you don't hear the players shouting because of the noise of the crowd. They were urged on by their coach, the assistant manager, who was almost strangling himself with the excitement, swearing at every kick, urging them on to greater effort, the reserves and first team alike, although he was a bit wary of upbraiding the firsts. That was the manager's preserve. But he did shout at Shug who went down with his usual display of Method-acting when Joe Pagan brought him down from behind.

'Get up, Gallacher. You fucking fairy.'

Shug was on the ground, managing to nurse a leg and make it look broken in at least three places. He waved his arms up and down at his side and then pretended to wave a wand. The first team sniggered. The assistant manager was furious.

'I know you're not hurt. Get up!'

The manager and the assistant continually stopped the game and made a kick or a corner be retaken, just to perfect the moves they'd been planning in the early sessions. All the players became strained and visibly upset when this happened, stopped short when their coitus had become interruptus, forced to suddenly remain still when all their bodies wanted to go on.

Right to the end, the reserves never let up. They went in to kill, not to take prisoners. The first team tried to remain aloof and casual throughout. They had red track-suit tops on while the reserves were in blue and somehow they looked so much more adult, more confident, more famous, even though I only knew one or two of them. Shug's was the only face which was passing famous. The reserves seemed spotty and adolescent, out of proportion with their hugely-developed thighs. Obscenely developed really, like a bathing beauty who'd been pumping glycerine into her breasts. That was the thing about Dennis Law. His thighs were in proportion, as slender as his body, quality not quantity. I knew for a fact that Joe Pagan was two years older than Shug and had been there all his life, yet he looked callow and thuggish. Being a reserve must make you a reserve, as being a film star makes you automatically a film star. But it must begin somewhere. Shug had done it, almost overnight. Perhaps he did have something special.

Across the grass from the pavilion came the groundsman, carrying pots of tea and paper cups. Shug saw him and broke away from the game, racing to be first. There must have been only seconds to go. But the assistant manager, who now had the whistle in his mouth, almost had apoplexy when he saw Shug leaving his game.

'Come back, Gallacher! Nobody leaves this pitch till I say so.'

Shug must have heard, but he kept running. He grabbed a cup of tea from the groundsman and lay on the ground, his back to the pitch. Everyone was staring at the assistant manager, wondering what he could do now, but hoping he would do it and settle Shug once and for all. The manager had missed the incident. He was at the far goal mouth, poking around with his feet, kicking the turf and looking at it, examining it carefully in his hand like a botanist, searching for specimens. When he saw that play had stopped, he moved back to the centre of the pitch, smiling at everyone, putting his arm round a few of his favourites in the first team and starting to walk with them towards the teapots.

'I hadn't finished,' said the assistant manager, contorted with fury. He hadn't acted quickly enough and now events had moved on without him.

'Oh, never mind,' said the manager agreeably. 'I think they've had enough for today. That wasn't half bad at all.'

Shug waved and smiled when he saw me, greeting me like a long lost friend. He put his arm round my shoulder and took me with him into the pavilion. The first team were getting undressed and showered first while the reserves hung around in an ante-room, the assistant manager haranguing them all on the things they'd done wrong. It was a very small pavilion, with only room for one team to get stripped off at a time. I stood around nervously, trying to avoid all the naked balls and cocks and thighs, but there wasn't anywhere else to look. I could see them studying me, wondering who this latest friend of Shuggy's was, but carefully ignoring me, making it clear I was an outsider and didn't belong amongst the naked flesh.

There's supposed to be a girl in the States who collects plaster casts of pop stars' erections. Someone could have a good time doing the same for football stars, but they probably wouldn't co-operate. They wouldn't be interested. For all their bulging manliness, there was something strangely unsexual about the scene.

Shug caught my eye and winked at me, as if he knew what I was thinking, which I was sure he didn't. I realised he'd done it deliberately, to give me a cheap thrill. I went out and waited for him outside the pavilion.

He went straight to my car when he was ready. They were there waiting for us, the gentlemen of the press, about half a dozen of them, reporters and photographers.

Shug was very good to them, chatting them along, referring to me as Stirling Moss, saying that he hoped they realised that my big end had been souped up. I didn't like him making jokes about me. All the cameramen laughed. I laughed too, ha ha ha.

Shug's agent had told them I was teaching him to drive. I said rubbish, but Shug agreed to let them write a big red L on a sheet of white paper and stick it on the front of my car. They said it would just look like two blokes in a car, otherwise.

'That's what you think, ducky,' said Shug, all winks. I'd been taken over. He'd lifted my part and my lines. He looked tanned, which I'd never noticed until then. He'd been so pale and white when he'd crept out of Glasgow. Yet the team hadn't been abroad. Just being famous had made him tanned.

I smiled for the photographers, deciding I might as well get in on the act. It was all harmless. My name wouldn't be used so they wouldn't find out who I was. It was all completely casual, teaching Shug to drive. He didn't even have a provisional licence. I only hoped Mr Innocent didn't object. He'd probably say I was running a driving school now, using his customers, pinched from him. I hoped there wasn't a law about pretending to be a driving instructor. We had enough trouble being unlicensed mini-cabs. The taxi drivers were always on about us not having to take exams, or do the knowledge and apply for a licence and all that.

'You get away quicker if you co-operate with the press,' said Shug as he drove away with me beside him. He accelerated far too quickly, just to show off, ruining my gear box. I warned him to drive carefully.

'You were pushing it a bit with that assistant manager,' I said.

'Who cares. He's just a thick cunt. Did you see him trying to tell me I shouldn't take shies. Telling me I should be on the park, running like fuck. If I'm nearest the ball, then sometimes it's obvious that a quick throw is the best thing. Just because he once played for England. Against Malta as well. You'd think he'd keep quiet about it.'

'That's something you'll never do.'

'Did you hear Alf Ramsey made enquiries about me, not realising I was Scottish?'

I didn't answer, trying to get him to concentrate on his driving.

'That's what Sammy told me. He's putting the story out tomorrow. So it must be true, mustn't it?'

He gave a big broad grin, so lovable, so young, so cheeky, so bloody near to a fall.

'You're not getting a Rolls are you?' I asked. I'd heard one of the reporters mentioning it to him.

'What do you think? Could do with one. Think of all the space on the back row. I can see the adverts now. At 50 mph, the only noise you can hear in Shug Gallacher's Rolls Royce is the throbbing of his organ.'

'I'd always thought you were impotent.'

'Ok, you can be my driver. I'll rig up a big rear mirror and you can watch every move. I'll do them all again in slow motion, for the action replays. You'd love that, wouldn't you. I know you're kinky.'

He grabbed at my balls, shouting and laughing. I had to lunge forward to take the steering wheel from his hands, just managing to right the car before we ran off the road. I stopped the car in a lay-by and told him not to be so stupid.

He settled down a bit after that. I felt so old compared with him. Off the field he was just a kid. He'd built up a lot of enmity from a section of the crowd, who thought he was just too cocky for words. He used to give them the V-sign back. He usually won them round in the end by an amazing piece of play. He had such utter confidence as a player that it never worried him. When he was complimented on a goal he'd agree, yes, it was rather brilliant. He'd never compliment a team they'd beaten but say they were useless. It was all to do with his age. That was how I excused him. If he ever lost his confidence as he got older, his play would surely suffer.

He drove quietly for a few miles, although he could hardly see because of his hair. He had let it go completely wild. On the field, despite what his critics said, it didn't affect his play as it was always streaming in the air behind him. But off the field, on TV or at home, he was constantly pushing it apart with his hands so that he could see out. It had gone off a lot as well, becoming stringier and scruffier the longer it got. I knew that everyone always mentioned it, so I never did.

He went serious and said that the jokes about the Rolls had begun to rebound. People really did now think he was loaded. He wasn't. If he ever passed his driving test, he probably wouldn't be able to afford a car at all. I was almost feeling sorry for him. Then in the next breath he was saying that Sammy was hoping to get him a free car from Ford. The stars of Chelsea, and some other teams, had become special sales reps. Their name went in the local papers and you contacted them if you wanted to buy a new car. You only had to turn up at the garage about once a month, sign a few forms, shake a few hands. Just the job.

'The only thing is,' he added, 'they haven't used any second-division stars yet.'

'So you're a second-division star,' I said.

'Watch it. You can go off some people. I was gonna give you a Cup Final ticket. I only get two. One each for my two special fans. You better not spoil yourself.'

He wasn't going to the Cup Final, so he said. He wasn't daft. He wouldn't watch football if he was paid. If he had absolutely nothing to do that afternoon he might watch it on the tele, but he doubted it. There was a beauty contest at Brighton which Sammy wanted him to judge. Just £20 for the afternoon's work, plus the perks.

I asked how Mrs Pagan was getting on. According to Shug she was now loving it, with kids and reporters at the door all day long who had to listen to her boring stories. He quite liked the idea of still living in his scruffy Kentish Town digs. Big star hasn't changed. But the real reason was that the club still wouldn't allow him to live on his own. If his new house ever got built, then things would come to a head. I thought his new house was all settled. He said no. They were all conning him, builders, electricians, agents. He hadn't paid the deposit yet. It was one of Sammy's publicity stunts which had been announced too soon. If he'd kept it quiet who he was, he might have got it a lot cheaper.

'And who are you?' I said.

Shug smiled. He was humming 'I beg your pardon', an awful pop song which he was making even worse by being unable to get the tune right. He was absolutely tone deaf, which he was very angry about. He felt he should be in touch and know all the songs. When he did pick up one he murdered it to death, going on and on. He didn't really believe that I thought it was awful. As he was driving, I didn't complain. I didn't want to spoil his concentration. He did a three-point turn, for once not going on the pavement, and felt very chuffed with himself, grinning his cocky grin. I said he should watch that. Everyone would see his yellow teeth.

'Jealous?' he said. It was hard to criticise Shug. He just never believed it. 'Do you think I'm worth £100,000?'

Spurs were now after him, so he'd heard. Ok, so Sammy had heard. Much better than going to Leeds. He couldn't stand the idea of going North again. He'd done all that bit. The only place was London. Even if Rangers, his boyhood idols, wanted him now he wouldn't go. If he did go to Spurs for £100,000 without asking for a transfer, he'd get five per cent of the deal, which would be £5,000, in his little hand. Not bad. A transfer every year and it would be worth staying in football.

'You mean instead of becoming Prime Minister,' I said.

Shug smiled this time and said nothing. Unlike Joff, he did appreciate other people's jokes. I suddenly realised we weren't heading back to Mrs Pagan's. We were now in Tufnell Park. He was pulling up outside Zak's house.

'I didn't know you still came here.'

'Every afternoon, when I feel like it. And I usually feel like it, every afternoon.'

I'd given him Zak's address weeks and weeks before. He'd thanked me but never went into details. I'd presumed that on becoming a big star, and with people like Sammy to fix him up, he'd long since moved on to smarter pads up the West End. All those big-busted starlets he was photographed with must have had their own flats.

He was out and into the block before I could ask him anything else. I watched him go up the staircase, reappearing and making a different funny face at every floor. Then at the top he disappeared. He couldn't be laying Sally, the sod. No, she was out with the baby on the Heath almost every afternoon. I'd seen her many times myself. There was only one person who was free every afternoon. Only people on the dole have nothing better to do.

8

The day of the murder was a Saturday. I was very busy all day, taking people backwards and forwards. I haven't got the order book to check on the people I took, but I'm sure even if I was given the names I would have forgotten what most of them looked like. Except for Zak, Shug and Joff.

But even they were just another job so the details aren't completely clear. In fact the thing I was worrying about most that day had nothing to do with any of them. It was the day I bought myself a track suit, the first in my life.

I went down to Camden Town in the morning, between jobs, as a change from sitting in the caff. It only cost £3 but when I rushed home to put it on I could see why. It was so baggy and the elastic practically castrated me. I cut it out and put new stuff in and it didn't look so bad. I took it off and found I was covered in blue down. I rushed to the mirror, convinced I'd got some sort of pox. It all came off in my hand and I realised it was with the track suit being new and cheap.

I'd bought a pair of running shoes as well, equally cheap. They were so new they looked like patent leather. I rather fancied myself in the proper gear. During the months I'd been playing football on Sunday mornings I'd been realising all the time that I just wasn't fit. What I needed was a run now and again during the week. I couldn't wait to go out and stun them for the first time on Sunday morning. So that Saturday I'd decided I'd finish early, however busy we were, and have a run on the Heath before dark.

But everybody in North London seemed to want us that day. A long-standing order in the book from four Burmese gentlemen was given to me at the last moment. Mr Innocent had decided to do two airports as he was on a diet. The Burmese wanted to go to Windsor and once you go on those trips, you get invited to eat and drink with them and it's churlish not to agree.

It was after the Burmese that I went for Zak. I hadn't known he'd booked a car till I came back from Windsor and saw it in the book.

They came out as if they were going up Mount Everest, loaded down with bags and balls and blankets and mounds of food. They were all going for a picnic tea. It was a lovely evening, but it was still a bit late for a picnic.

'I couldn't go before the results came through, could I,' said Zak. He was wearing the clothes I'd first seen him in, jeans and his worn-out blue plimsolls. But Sally and the kids were dressed to kill, all in new outfits.

'The full Hampstead bit,' she said. 'We'll get mixed up with the Kenwood open-air concert, so we've got to look the part.'

I cut my fingers jamming the baby's push-chair in the boot. The other two insisted that they held every ball and bat on their knees in the back of the car. Sally was loaded down with rings, the cheap sort, but huge and very arty. I noticed that Zak was almost naked, no ornaments and hardly any clothes. When it got cold, he'd be frozen in his T shirt.

'I'm going to do some running after the picnic,' he said, clapping his hands like a cheer leader, jumping up and down, letting me and Sally get the kids and the stuff into the car. He was very cocky.

'Must get fit for tomorrow, you know. You got your track suit yet?'

'Got it today. I thought about driving in it, but I didn't want to spoil the creases.'

'I've got mine ordered, and a pair of real boots. I'm getting them in white, like Alan Ball.'

During the drive we discussed the afternoon's matches then I remembered about his TV programme. How had it gone?

'Which TV programme?'

'Joff's,' I said. 'You and he seemed to get on like a house on fire.'

He looked annoyed, as if I was cross-examining him, trying to trick him. He'd got into the car so bouncy and jokey. I'd never seen him so gay, or the family. It was almost as if he'd got a job. I didn't want to ask him that. Sally would tell me if he had. When you're on the dole, it gets a bit draggy having to tell people all the time.

'Stop playing with that ball!' he shouted to his boys in the back, all bad tempered.

'Can we have the sandwiches now?' they both shouted, pulling their mother's face to make her look at them.

'You've just come out of the house, for goodness' sake.'

'We want them now.'

'You'll make a mess of Franko's lovely car.' said Sally.

'I don't care,' I said. 'Go right ahead. People have made worse messes.'

'What a daft reason to give them,' said Zak, now turning on Sally. 'Tell them the picnic is at Kenwood, not here.'

'You tell them. You're their father.'

They were half-way through two sandwiches and were struggling to open a plastic bottle of orange juice, with a wedge of cake in each hand, ready for the first gap in their eating.

'Mum, can we have an ice cream in Kenwood, Mum? Can we?'

'I've no money,' said Sally. 'Your Dad's got all the money.'

There were cars parked for miles along the road to Kenwood. A notice on both gates said no entry, but I drove through regardless and took them right up to the front door, as if it was the Mayor of Camden himself.

Zak wasn't speaking to Sally. He let me unload all the gear and stood there running on the spot.

'Ok then?' he said to Sally, getting out the money to pay me. She piled everything onto the pram and started across the flower garden to the wilder bit, away from the music. The kids were screaming that they wanted to hear the music, and where was Dad going, and what about the ice cream, and they were hungry, they wanted a wee wee, they wanted to go home, now.

'See you then,' said Zak, bounding off towards the woods.

I thought about forgetting my other jobs and helping Sally and the kids. I liked her very much. Sally had a nice mixture of kindness and sharpness. She didn't go along with half of Zak's crackpot layabout philosophies. She'd told me many a time that if she was him, she would definitely have got a job years ago, however draggy. She couldn't have stuck being on the dole with such responsibilities. But she also admitted that if Zak was the sort of person who'd have been content with a safe little nine-to-five job, then in that case Zak wouldn't be the sort of person she'd want to live with. She found his attitudes refreshing and stimulating. The only trouble was the reality. That was beginning to get her down.

I had to rush to get to the ground in time. I'd taken too long with Zak and Co. Ten minutes earlier would have made all the difference, but now I'd caught the crowds coming away and they were blocking the street. I had to crawl forward, blaring my horn, literally pushing people with my bumpers. One skinhead put his arm through the window and caught me right on the ear. There was a slight opening ahead and I accelerated, throwing him off. I closed all the windows and edged forward again. The crowds were sullen and depressed. They'd obviously been well and truly hammered. I could hear Shug's name on lots of lips, all of them seemed to be saying Bloody Useless. They should let him go. He's gone right off.

They were all hurrying to get home, silently, each with his own thoughts, wanting the day, the week-end, to be over till next week. My presence, going the wrong way, made them furious. I feared for the car. I could hear their fists battering on the back and on the roof as I went past. I just needed to knock some yobbo too hard and they'd have me, boots through the windscreen and I'd be on the floor, trampled to death. I eased round a corner and came upon a hot dog stall completely wrecked. A gang of skinheads were racing away, led by a boy with a swastika on his back. Their brown boots were banging on the pavements, shouting and yelling, looking for something or someone else to wreck. A young boy, covered in blood, who could only have been about thirteen, was in tears, wiping his face on his white jacket, trying to pick up piles of soggy onions. Everybody was edging past him, not getting involved, not wanting to be the Samaritan. At the back of the crowd I saw Ginger, the kid I sometimes played football with on the Heath, but I couldn't tell if he was with the skinhead gang.

I thought about remaining stationary, waiting till the crowds had gone, but I was still a sitting target, jammed in the middle of the road, surrounded by a sea of people. It would be a horrible way to die, devoured by an angry gang simply because they were looking for someone to pick on, someone who annoyed them. It could be done so quickly, like the hot dog stall. They'd up-turn the car, break the windows, beat me up and be away, into the crowds.

At last, the crowds began to thin out. I was only twenty minutes late after all, though it had seemed an eternity. Shug was at the players' entrance, signing autographs, but looking very tired. He pushed them away when he saw me and got in quickly, followed by Sammy, his awful agent.

'It was that big bastard. I saw him go for you in the first minute,' said Sammy. 'You didn't have a chance. He should have been sent right off. It was diabolical.'

'Oh shut up,' said Shug.

'And as for that bloody referee. Giving a free kick to them and taking your name. The whole bloody crowd saw what that big bastard had done.'

'I started it. He got away with it. That's all there is to it. Now belt up. You're giving me a headache.'

I drove in silence. They were both in the back, Sammy all belligerent and indignant, Shug all drained, sullen and thoughtful.

'Anyway, I've got you down as a judge at Brighton tomorrow. Lots of talent.'

'I'm not going.'

'Oh for Chrissake. I thought we turned down the Big Match because of Brighton?'

'I'm not doing that either.'

'You'll feel better tomorrow. I won't cancel it yet.'

'Do what you like.'

'Now now, Shuggy, boy. It's what *you* like. If you don't wanna meet those birds, don't meet those birds.'

'Shut up! Franko. Can you drive to Zak's please.'

'He's not in,' I said, 'I've just taken them on the Heath.'

'What? Oh, Christ.'

'Hold it, hold it, Shuggy. We've got our date. At Jack Straw's. Remember? To discuss that TV deal. We can't get out of that. You promised. He'll be there already. Remember?'

Sammy was all open hands, pleading almost, but from a position of strength and he knew it. Shug was cursing, but whatever it was, even he knew he couldn't get out of it.

'You said you'd go,' said Sammy, all leers. 'It's what you want. Take you out of yourself. There's no going back now.'

Shug sighed and Sammy smiled. Then Sammy turned to me, his smiles and pleading disappearing.

'Stop farting around, driver. We want Jack Straw's fast. You've already made us an hour late.'

'I'm not sure I want to be taken out of myself,' said Shug slowly.

Sparkle was out on the pavement, looking for me when I got back. I'd thought about going straight home and having my run on the Heath, even though I wasn't officially off for another half hour. You never get nice short jobs when you want them. I tried to avoid her. It was probably those four Burmese blokes who wanted to go back to Windsor for their plastic macs. They'd left them in a caff and had worried all the way home.

'Thank goodness I've got you,' said Sparkle. 'Urgent job for you. Mr Innocent said at all costs you had to do it. Now I can go home.'

'Hard cheese. So can I.'

'You can't! It's Mr Howard. He rang half an hour ago. I wrote it in the book, see. He's waiting for you at Portland Square. The BBC.'

'You're getting very efficient,' I said. 'Writing down quick jobs like that. I thought Mr Innocent told us only to put day-ahead jobs in the book, so the accountant can't see how much work we're doing.'

'I don't know anything about that,' she said, all priggish. 'All I know is he's waiting, this minute.'

'Where's he going?'

'Ooh. I forgot to ask.'

'Typical,' I said, slamming out of the office.

I presumed he wanted to be brought home, as usual, so there was no need to take my bad temper out on Sparkle.

For once, Joff was waiting for me when I arrived. He closed the car door with a bang and got in beside me. He'd been doing a broadcast, helping out the steam chaps. He was clutching a fat document case which he carried everywhere with him, just to let you see what a high-powered bloke he was. He maintained it was made of elephant's testicles. He'd shot the elephant himself when he'd been on a programme in Africa. A taxidermist in Kentish Town had made it for him. The feet were used as wastepaper baskets. I didn't answer. I knew most of Joff's stories off by heart. The only interest was in seeing how he improved them.

I asked how Eddie was. Joff said he was much better now he was home. Those bloody nurses didn't understand at all. All it took was a loving hand. I asked facetiously if he'd got a home help.

'Cheeky,' said Joff, all smiles, patting me on the knee. He was in high good humour. He must have something lined up.

He then started to tell me a story I hadn't heard before. All about how he had studied at Barts for some time. He would have been a brilliant doctor. Everyone said so. His father after all had been a world-famous surgeon. I said that he'd found better ways of cutting up people than being a surgeon. He agreed. You couldn't insult Joff like that. One of his images of himself, apart from being debonair and smooth and kind to animals, was of the ruthless interrogator and champion of truth who was fearless in his treatment of villains.

I asked how his wife was getting on. He hadn't mentioned her recently. He said there had been absolute silence from her and the solicitors. He'd asked to see his son Toby, but they'd refused.

'That's what happens when you get married to a bitch. She says she won't let me see him again. I'm a bad influence or some such rubbish.'

To change the conversation, I started to tell him about my track suit, but he wasn't listening. He was usually very keen on my private life so normally I didn't tell him anything. He did it in a cold disinterested way, researching a subject, looking for angles rather than flesh and blood.

He'd just had his hair cut, I could tell. He always had it brushed forward, trying hard to disguise the bald patches at the sides. He had a little quiff at the top, as if his mother had put it in for him, or Eddie. Eddie was always going on at him to grow his sideboards and his hair. He wasn't all that old. But Joff was very conscious of his BBC position. He went to great pains to appear straight and conventional, especially when it came to things like living with Eddie. No one at the BBC knew about it, not even Caroline.

When we got into Hampstead I started turning towards his square but he said no, go straight on up Heath Street. He had a date at Jack Straw's. Important business. I said I knew all about it. He was meeting Shuggy.

'Who?' he said. 'I don't know anyone called Shuggy. It's an agent called Freeman, some con man with a stable of footballers. That's all I know. He's got an idea for a sports quiz.'

'That'll be Sammy Freeman,' I said. 'Good friend of mine. I took them there almost an hour ago. They'll probably have gone by now.'

'Oh Christ. Is it that late?'

He was all bad tempered, partly because I knew about his business. He liked to think he was constantly involved in high-powered secret negotiations. I didn't care. I was in a hurry to get rid of him and go for my run.

It was crowded round White Stone Pond. There was a gang of yobboes going across the crossing, singing and waving red and white scarves, taking as much time as they could. They got across and ran down the slopes of the Heath. I recognised Ginger and one or two others.

I drew up outside Jack Straw's. I hoped Shuggy and Sammy had gone. It would serve Joff right.

9

The next morning, Sunday morning, the day I saw the body, I woke so early I was up and dressed without waiting for Gran to bring me my morning tea. For some reason I didn't feel sleepy. Perhaps it was the excitement of it being a beautiful fresh May morning. I decided to creep out in my track suit and gently warm up before the match without anyone seeing me. My run the previous night had been disastrous. I'd collapsed after ten minutes. I now wanted to try that Canadian army method where you jog a little bit then walk a little bit. That sounded more my style, especially the walking.

I walked up Parliament Hill, ready to jog should I meet anyone, but the Heath was deserted. I hadn't been up so early since I used to deliver newspapers, and even then Sunday was always a late day.

Behind a tree I came across a couple of hippies, asleep on a blanket, a guitar between them, smiling serenely. They were a bit early. It wasn't that hot. By mid August you can't get moving for people sleeping out on the Heath, couples coupling, rapists resting, exhibitionists arranging their raincoats for another hard day's exposure.

I sat on a slope looking towards Highgate. From that angle it always looks like an incredibly green village on the hills of the Côte d'Azur. When you penetrate that sloping village it's just another chunk of suburbia.

When I was a kid there used to be a man who stood on top of Parliament Hill with a telescope. He charged kids a penny a time to look through it, but if he was in a good mood and he liked you, he'd let you look through it for nothing. You saw amazing things. Then one day the police took him away. While the little innocents had been peering through his telescope his hands had been up their little shorts. Poor fellow. I wonder where he is now. I thought he was nice.

I sat on a bench beside the first pond, the Submarine Pond as we always used to call it. Some kids once told me, one day in 1945, that they'd seen a Nazi submarine, periscope and all, emerging from the water. They said it had come underground, using the subterranean River Fleet which is supposed to run from Highgate Ponds under the streets down to the Thames. Being four, I believed it all. So did my Gran. I wanted to tell the Home Guard men who manned the barrage balloon on the Heath, but she wouldn't let me. She believed Hitler had spies everywhere and if we wanted to keep alive, you told nothing to nobody.

There was nothing happening in the Submarine Pond. It was the close season for fishing, until 15 June. I moved on to the next pond, the Swimming Pond, to see if anyone was around. That's the one with the diving board so high that if you dive off it into the water, you'll never come up again. So I used to be told. Nobody was diving. The third pond, the Boat Pond, was also deserted, which was strange. There was usually some idiot desperately trying to get his miniature speed boat to work, tugging at the starting cord between his legs.

The fourth pond is the Wild Pond because it's fenced off to protect the birds and wild life. You're never allowed to fish there, even in the season. We used to, of course, posting one kid to look for the parkies.

In the middle of the Wild Pond was a rowing boat. I'd never seen a rowing boat on the Wild Pond before. I'd never thought it was deep enough. I'd seen boats on each of the other three ponds at some time. There was always one on the Swimming Pond. In the season they're supposed to have a parkie continuously rowing round to stop them having it off in the water.

There was a parkie in the rowing boat in the middle of the Wild Pond but I didn't recognise him. At one time I knew them all. Against the railings, waiting for him, were another three park keepers. They all had hooks and were digging and slashing at the reeds. They looked cold and menacing, slashing away abstractedly in the morning mist which hung a few feet over the water.

They were hardly looking at what they were doing. Any wild life wouldn't have a chance against them.

I got near to them and could hear them talking. One was saying to the other that he didn't care about last week. Spurs were going to shit on Arsenal. They suddenly looked at me, defiantly, accusingly, as if I'd been spying on them. Then they looked away. Just another daft runner, trudging round the Heath with nothing better to do.

I asked one of them what they were looking for. He looked at me then looked away, telling the others that they could do what they liked, but he was going for tea. A bloke with a slobbering mouth arrived. He spent all his life in his track suit, panting round and round. He was a pleasant bloke, even if his grunts seemed frightening. The two remaining parkies cheered up. A bit of sport. They asked him about his sex life. Was he getting enough? The usual stuff. One of them reminded the other about a dog they'd found that morning. Perhaps Zatopek had been interfering with it. They both laughed.

'Ugh, ugh, not me,' grunted Zatopek. 'Last night. In the bushes. In the corner, ugh ugh . . .'

'Oh give over,' said one parkie and they both returned to slashing at the reeds.

Perhaps it was just something silly, like a kid's toy which had been lost, one of those speed boats. Why shouldn't they be their normal selves.

A woman arrived with three dogs. They stood at the side of the railings, barking at the boat in the middle, while the woman shouted at them in a high pitched posh voice to stop it, at once. She was furious at having to stop beside the two park keepers, deliberately taking no notice of what they were doing.

Across the pond through the willows I could see a strange line of people coming along the little road which leads into Millfield Lane. They were all in black, slowly trudging one behind the other, carrying strange-shaped hoes and long-handled spades over their shoulders. A line of peasants coming from their mediaeval fields. As they passed the end of the pond I could hear them talking to each other in a language I didn't understand. They were gnarled and weather-beaten and looked straight out of the Siberian Steppes. Or the BBC casting department. I looked round for any film cameras. The Heath that morning did have an unusual feeling, either by nature or intent. It might all be a play. After sex maniacs, film crews make up a big part of the Heath's summer migrants. But no one else was watching. Perhaps it was a demonstration in search of an audience.

'Bloody Russians,' said one of the parkies. They were Russians going back to the residence. I'd forgotten it was so near. They must have been working all night in their allotments. Or pretending to work in their allotments.

There was the sound of girlish shouts and yells in the distance. The men in the compound beside their swimming pool must have started their early morning badminton. I could hear the shuttle-cock clicking back and forth, a funny bird-like noise, clean and final. I wondered if they were all naked or if they'd put their sexy little loincloths on. I hadn't been inside the compound for years. All that pickled walnut flesh gives me the creeps. I wouldn't mind if any of them were pretty but they're mostly about 150.

The two parkies were now leaning on their hooks, bored and fed up. I'd made a mistake. Nothing was going to happen. It had been a routine job. Cleaning the weeds. Giving the fish a chance to breathe. Even Zatopek had got fed up and restarted his run.

I walked slowly up the hill towards Kenwood. I went through the wood to the coach house to have a cup of tea but it was closed.

I came back the same way, which was unusual for me. I have a fetish about having circular walks. From the exit to the wood I could see a crowd had gathered beside the Wild Pond. The rowing boat was no longer in the middle. In the distance I heard a police siren. Down Millfield Lane came a police car followed by an ambulance, their lights flashing and sirens screaming. I ran back down the hill. I couldn't understand where all the people had come from.

The park keeper who'd been rowing the boat was now at the side – trying to pull something out of his boat, helped by the two parkies with hooks. I tried to edge my way to the front to see what was happening; but there were so many people and dogs jammed against the fence that I couldn't get a proper view.

Police and ambulance men raced from their vehicles carrying blankets. One blanket was thrown over the head and all I could see was the body as it was dragged out of the boat. A perfect body, tough and muscular, young and fit-looking, naked and unmarked, except for signs of blood round the neck. From the neck hung a pendant on a silver chain, undamaged. I couldn't see whether it was a crucifix or a St Christopher medal. There were no rings on his fingers. I always look at people's hands. I hate mine. They're so short and ugly. His hands were strong and masculine.

The ambulance men quickly wrapped the rest of the blankets round the body. It was hoisted up like a sack of potatoes which had gone to seed, all sluggish and soggy, and into the ambulance.

The crowd drew back from the fence to watch the ambulance drive away. As soon as it had disappeared, they began to disperse. I stood beside the parkies as they calmly cleaned their hooks, wiped the boat down and made good the damage to the sides of the pond. One said to the other that it was more interesting than clearing up the dog muck.

I stood looking at the pond, hoping for some sign, but none came. The ducks had come back and were chasing each other in the reeds. If questioned, they would deny all knowledge of what had happened. A magic cloth had wiped away the scene completely.

10

On Monday morning I went up to Hampstead High Street and bought the first edition of the *Evening Standard* at the Tube station. I tore it open only to find acres of racing tips and starters. I asked the newsvendor for the real paper, the one you could read, and he said that was it till midday.

I went to the Coffee Cup and sat outside in the sun and carbon monoxide fumes and turned over the pages, looking for reading fodder. Beside me two foreign journalists were going on about some demonstration they'd been at the day before at the Russian Embassy, boasting about some spy scandal they were about to uncover. At another table a film director was boring some girl about a part he was going to give her, when the backing came through.

The Londoner's Diary was absolutely dateless, stories that must have been lying growing yellow at the edges for centuries. I suppose over the week-end they have a hard struggle to fill it up. Their lead story was about an ex-debutante getting engaged. There was an old smudgy photograph and it had an inky line through it, a crease in the paper where my copy had stuck in the presses.

I looked again at the debutante's fat podgy face and I suddenly realised it was Caroline. Caroline Stark-Boncers, so it said. It was the first time I'd read in a newspaper about someone I knew. I wanted to tell the director, or even the journalists. I felt excited, as if I'd had a fright. I clicked my tongue and said well, well, the way they do in Hampstead coffee bars to draw attention to themselves, but no one turned round.

The bloke she was getting engaged to was Jonathan Howard, the well-known TV personality. I really did shout aloud at that, without meaning to. 'Romance for ex-deb secretary', said the headline. The writer, having listed Caroline's boring connections, mainly a couple of Hons, then tried to get some fun at her expense for boasting that she was engaged to a bloke who was already married. 'When Joff's divorce comes through, we're getting married right away. Joff is short for Jonathan. I fell in love with him from the beginning.' Even Caroline wouldn't have come out with such rubbish. It must have been put in her mouth. All it said about Jonathan was that he was unavailable for comment last night. It was a non-story as far as most readers were concerned. But I wondered what Eddie would think of it.

Joff always boasted he would have a go at anything, as long as it moved, but I wouldn't have touched Caroline with half a dozen barge poles, which is what you would have needed for Caroline. But some people prefer them fat. I'd never heard Joff express any preferences in that line. His big thing was sweat. He hated girls, and boys, who shaved under their arms or between their legs. It spoiled seventy-five per cent of the sensation. Caroline was absolutely crazy about him. Joff was a snob. So perhaps he was attracted by her connections, and her sweat.

With wondering about the Caroline story I almost forgot what I'd bought a paper for in the first place. I went right through it again from the beginning, reading every little paragraph. There was nothing about a body being discovered on the Heath.

I didn't get any free time till much later in the day. Wondering if Eddie had seen the news about Joff and Caroline, I bought the final edition of the *Standard*, though it might seem bitchy taking it to him, as if I was gloating over his misfortune. If I'd been Eddie, I would have considered it a blessed relief. A bloke with his looks could easily get another fellow. He was too good for Joff. But they had seemed very fond of each other. Poor lad. It was just the sort of dirty trick Joff would do behind his back. I wouldn't have liked to have been dumped for Caroline.

I drew up at the end of the square, the way we were supposed to, and opened the *Standard* to have a last look at the story, in case they had any more information. It wasn't there. It hadn't even been cut down to a paragraph and put at the end. It had disappeared completely.

Eddie welcomed me with open arms and pressed me to sit down and have a quiet sherry, he was just having one. He had on a cashmere polo neck and purple corduroy trousers. He looked as if he was waiting for someone and was all excited.

'I'm *so* glad you've come. It's been go go go all evening, polishing and scrubbing. I haven't had a minute's rest.'

He burbled on and then asked me why I was so depressed. He'd seen me in the car, furiously turning over the pages of the evening paper. I said it was nothing. I hadn't made the England team once again. I was getting used to it.

'I've bought four copies today,' he said, getting up and taking a pile of papers from beneath a pouffe. 'This story wasn't in the last edition. Look. The bastards dropped it.'

As I hadn't mentioned Joff's engagement first, I had to read the story and register surprise, which was very hard. I could hear my exclamations ringing completely false.

'Isn't it great? I do hope she's read it. The buggers. If only they'd kept it in all day. It was all my idea. Another sherry?'

Eddie explained that Joff's wife had been making trouble again

and the solicitors' letters had been flying back and forth. To prove
to the world, and to the BBC, that Joff was a straight-up-and-down
heterosexual Eddie had decided Joff should become engaged to
someone, and who better than Caroline. She didn't know, alas,
that it was all a plot. Joff had been worried that he might have to
sleep with Caroline but Eddie had pointed out she was a Christian.
No pre-marital relations. They'd have to wait, panting, until he
was divorced.

Eddie was thrilled with his little self. Not only did it disprove
any nasty scandal about Joff, which apparently his wife was trying
to spread, it also made Joff a fit and proper person to have access
to his own child. If he was known to be bent, said Eddie, no judge
would ever let him get his hands on Toby, his eleven-year-old kid.
I was already lost in all the complications. But I said great, very
clever, he'd get in the OBE list at this rate.

'Where is he anyway?' I asked carefully.

'He's gone to Tangiers. He's got a lead on Martin Bormann, but
don't tell anyone. He's rung me to say the official story is now Birmingham, just in case any ITV people hear about it. Somebody's
trying to sell an exclusive interview with him. Joff's been offered it
first.'

Eddie offered me another sherry but I said no. I didn't like drinking on an empty stomach. In that case, said Eddie, stay for dinner.
I hadn't meant that. I rose to go but he insisted. He'd bought two
beautiful filet steaks for Joff's coming back. Now he wasn't coming
back for another two days. He didn't want to waste them. I rang
Mr Innocent to say I wasn't working that evening. Then I accepted
another sherry.

Eddie asked if I minded not having potatoes. He was slimming.
I said fine, I was in training. He asked if I liked taramasalata. He'd
made some a couple of days ago and there was still a bit left. I said
I'd never had it.

'Now's your chance,' he said. 'You've got to take your chances
when you can.'

'Why?' I said. He was making a dressing for the salad. Gran got
hers out of a Heinz bottle. Eddie had jars and bottles everywhere
plus garlic, lemon and something he said was called basil.

'Because life is nothing without experiences. It's only through experiences that you find out who you are.'

'Oh yes,' I said. 'I've never had basil.'

I felt so much younger than him, being silly and flippant when he was being sensible and mature. He was only about twenty yet he was so calm and at ease. I was trying to hide all my insecurities with daft remarks.

I asked about Joff. He said Joff lived in a dream world where he was always doing earth-shattering stories which the whole world was waiting for, like this stupid trip to Tangiers. His enemies, naturally, were after him so his motives and his movements were always very complicated. He had only one real enemy, himself. If he came to terms with that one he'd be so much happier.

Over the meal, he said he wasn't worried about Joff's promiscuity. Joff worried about it more than he did. If Joff felt like a one-night stand, fine. He preferred staying at home. When the time came when he didn't feel like staying at home, he'd go out. It was all this soul searching he didn't like. It was a right drag.

He was in the Civil Service. I laughed and he was rather hurt. Why shouldn't he be? He could show me his three A-levels, if I wanted to see them. It was a perfectly respectable job with a sound future. He'd have hated anything artistic. That was a rat race, unless you were brilliant. It was life that mattered, not work.

'I thought you were a hairdresser when you came to the door that first time,' he said. 'Or someone from the gas board doing natural gas conversions. They all look like hairdressers.'

I told him about the time I had been a hairdresser, but not about Johnny. Something held me back. I didn't want to think about him. But it suddenly struck me that I'd never liked Johnny in any way. Being bent was nothing to do with it, yet I'd held that against him. I liked Eddie as a human being. Just to prove it, I offered to wash up. He said no, there was a dish washer. Joff didn't let him use it when he was on his own. Joff was so bloody mean. He checked every housekeeping bill to make sure Eddie wasn't over-spending.

I had a brandy afterwards, Joff's best, which Eddie wasn't supposed to touch. We played a few records, chatted, messed around. He said stay for cocoa. He always had some. I was scared he might say stay the night. I said no. Gran would be waiting. She'd be out in the street, shouting my name.

'Thanks for a smashing meal,' I said as I got quickly into my car.

'Lovely to have you,' said Eddie, smiling.

II

I spent several days trying to contact Shug. Each time I rang his digs I got Joe Pagan, who said he didn't know nuffink. I couldn't get Mrs Pagan, who would have been the best person. She was in hospital. I rang the club in the end, with a long story about being his regular driver and wanting to know where he was. They were idiots on the switchboard. First of all they said they weren't allowed to divulge players' home addresses. I said I knew his home address. I was his driver, wasn't I. Then they said he'd gone on the club's summer tour. I said when. She checked, and came back and said sorry, it hadn't started yet. Then she remembered. He'd gone home to Glasgow. His mother was ill.

There had been a small paragraph in Tuesday's evening papers saying the body of a well-built man had been found on the Heath over the week-end. The police were investigating. Since then, there had been no other news. I'd gone back to thinking about more important things, like inviting myself to another of Eddie's meals or speculating on Mr Innocent's sex life. Sparkle had been giving me coy hints about his prowess. I wondered if he'd discovered her.

On Friday, Shuggy contacted me. An envelope arrived out of the blue, a plain brown envelope containing one ticket. I recognised his spastic sprawl immediately.

I'd completely forgotten about Wembley since he'd mentioned it weeks ago. I'd thought it was one of his usual Big Mick gestures. I hadn't even reminded him of his promise, though several times I'd taken him backwards and forwards to the ground. He was taking a big chance, sending it to me so near the day of the match. I might never have got it in time. Perhaps something had happened at the last minute, a friend had let him down. I wondered who the other special friend would be.

I went part of the way to Wembley by car, parking at Finchley Road and then got the Tube the rest of the way to Wembley Park. I looked up the avenue, broad and triumphant, with Wembley's rounded towers at the bottom, searching for a face I knew. Out of 100,000 I must know someone, especially the someone I was expecting to meet.

There seemed to be salesmen everywhere, selling ices and hot dogs and hamburgers as well as pennants, flags and toys. The crowd was very good natured, singing and chanting, the rival gangs taunting each other, but no one being nasty. They were even taking leaflets from The End of the World Is At Hand people. The sun must have brought them out. One of them had a car parked at the side with a loudspeaker rigged up, trying to attract the crowd by shouting out that the Great Referee in the Sky had the hardest job of all.

At the sides, on the grass verges, there were families, dusty and dirty, who looked as if they'd been camping there since the last Cup Final. My ticket said I had to go in by the E turnstiles and then head for my seat, Row J, number 64. I wondered if the person I was going to meet was J65 or J63.

Round the iron grilles beside entrance E there were gangs of lads, some sitting on the worn grass, some standing against the rails, waiting, like animals, to pounce on anyone displaying his ticket. A policeman was trying to control the ones who had got tickets, moving them into a line. I was too scared to examine mine. I wanted to, even though I'd memorised the number. Behind me the TV camera crews on top of parked cars were doing the crowd scenes, talking earnestly into microphones, surrounded by gangs of young kids, all waving and trying to get in on the picture.

I felt very relieved when I got inside, safe from the hordes. I got lost at first, trying to find my seat, and trudged down several dark grey concrete corridors. Then suddenly this incredible green loomed up from the end of what seemed a dark tunnel and hit me in the eyes, an oasis of perfect turf. The sun was shining, the crowds were singing, and the atmosphere was exciting me so that I felt I could rise up and float down into the bowl and be perfectly safe. Seats number 63 and 65 J, on either side of me, were empty.

Whoever was coming to sit beside me, in 63 or 65, would obviously be staying quite a while, for 90 minutes at least. The pitch was covered in hurdles and jumps and boring dogs, part of some display which was being put on to entertain the crowds. I decided to go for a drink. The first part of my mission had been accomplished. I'd got there in one piece.

When I got back to my seat, there was a helicopter hovering overhead. Probably full of Sunday-newspaper men, looking for scoops. Or police, waiting to see who was going to join me in seat J63 or 65.

The dogs disappeared and a Guards band marched out, determined to delight the crowds. A bloke in a white jacket climbed on a make-shift dais and tried to conduct the crowd in the community singing, but they were too busy singing their own team songs. They stopped singing at last when the teams came out. They went mad instead. The National Anthem was played for the Duke of Kent who shook hands with the teams. I stood up with everyone else, not wanting to be conspicuous.

Arsenal gave away four nasty fouls in succession and the Liverpool fans were furious. A very fat man was pushing his way down the aisle towards me, annoying everyone, just as one of the free kicks was about to be taken. He stopped, waiting for the excitement to die away again. I couldn't see who it was, but if it was the person I feared it was, I was going straight home. The fat man moved forward again – and went right past me.

I hadn't noticed there was anyone in his lee, letting him do the pushing. She had long blonde hair, falling thick round her face and a beautiful long purple maxi dress. She sat down quietly beside me and I almost jumped with the surprise. It was Sally, Zak's wife. She didn't look at me but glanced up and down at her programme, identifying the players, working out what was happening.

I turned to look at her but she gave no sign that she knew me. Down below, in the green bowl in front of us, they were all stiff and slow and nervous, as if the grass was too deep for them and pulling at their legs. I wanted to say to Sally that I bet it looks better on TV. Kennedy was presented with what seemed an open goal for Arsenal. I leaned forward in my seat, hoping he'd miss it. As Spurs is my team, I definitely didn't want Arsenal to win. I felt a hand take hold of my right hand and squeeze it. I turned to Sally and she was smiling at me, handing me a packet of chewing gum.

She said it had taken her an hour and a half to get there. She'd gone into town to get a Tube out and it had been like a battlefield. I said I'd take her home. I was explaining to her where I'd parked and how clever I'd been, but two blokes behind pushed me and told me to shut up and keep still. Sally smiled at me and held my hand again.

I hate it when you're supposed to chase girls, to try and get your hands up them, even though I know that's what blokes are supposed to do and it's what girls are supposed to like. I prefer gentle, natural responses, male or female, whoever it is, a coming together with no strings attached, not part of a ritualised sex game, each person selling a bit of him or herself before going on to the next stage in the game. Sally's hands felt real. Or was I excited by the thought of what she knew?

She said that Shuggy had promised to take her to the match, but that at the last moment he'd decided to go home and see his mother in Glasgow who was ill. Sally herself had posted my letter, having failed to get me on the phone. I said it was lucky for me.

We had a drink at half time and I asked her how long she'd been interested in football. Only since the arrival of Shuggy. She'd found a lot of new interests, since the arrival of Shuggy. I wasn't sure what that was supposed to mean. I asked about Zak and she was very non-committal. He'd gone to Newcastle, his home town, to look for a job. One of his many crazy ideas. As if Newcastle, of all places, didn't have its own unemployment problem. They'd got married up there. She certainly wouldn't go back, even if he did find a job.

The second half was almost as boring as the first, though Sally went on as if it was really great. These new converts to football tend to overdo it. I was going off her a bit, with all her affected enthusiasm. She couldn't help her middle-class voice. But like girls swearing, shouting and roaring just didn't seem feminine. I was already thinking about full time, wondering what I'd do with her when I drove her home. She'd already told me she'd got rid of the kids for the week-end, down to her mother's in Alfriston. She'd arranged it weeks ago, thinking Shuggy was going to be at home. I don't know how I ever thought that Shug and Zak were both bent.

When Steve Heighway scored in extra time I asked her if she fancied him. I said I did. He looked super. She agreed. She'd been panting for him ever since she saw him on Panorama. She loved athletic men. I asked her why she didn't come to watch us on Sunday mornings. I was quite a goer myself, when I got myself going.

Extra time turned out to be worth the rest of the match put together. We were both clutching each other with the tension, hoping Liverpool would hold out. She hated Arsenal because Shuggy did. My head was aching with the excitement. We stayed behind at the end, till the worst of the crowds had gone.

I helped her out of the terraces, my arm round her, steering her away from the worst of the crowds. I'd never been so intimate with a young blonde for years. I wouldn't have minded meeting Mr Innocent, just to ruin all his jokes at my expense.

The End of the World was still no Nigher, except for Liverpool fans, but the loudspeaker was still going. I bought two hamburgers, passing one to her. She held it between two fingers till she came to a waste bin, then she dropped it in, shuddering.

'How can you? It's absolutely disgusting.'

It was all coming back to me, those little experiments years ago. They will try to impose their likes and dislikes on you. Then try to make you feel a heel, loathsome, repellant, not fit to touch the hairs of their maiden, as if anyone would want to, not in their right mind anyway. The very thought of it put me off. We were both sweaty and dirty. I knew how I felt. I didn't want to know how she felt. We didn't speak again till we got on the Tube.

She put her arm round me as we sat together, jammed in tightly. She whispered in my ear that she would come and watch me play tomorrow morning. She'd watch me any time, doing anything. She sniggered. I wasn't sure if she was poking fun at me. She was probably putting it all on, feeling safe.

Under the arm that she had round me there was a great dark tide-mark of sweat. I tried to move her arm down but I couldn't. I recognised one of the blokes in the Tube. He was an Arsenal fan, the worse for wear and sipping from a hip flask. He was winking at me, nudging his mates. Football, a drink, only one thing missing. Some blokes had all the luck. He could have her. I looked the other way.

We got to her flat and she asked me if I'd like a drink. She had a half bottle of Spanish chablis, all lovely and cold in the fridge. Wouldn't you like to slip into something cool, she said. I tried to remember a joke, but as usual I couldn't. She then opened a bottle of Algerian Beaujolais, but said naughty naughty, we'd have that with the meal, spaghetti bolognaise. She'd got it all ready that morning. There was only the spaghetti to boil. I said Mr Innocent was expecting me. Fuck Mr Innocent, she said, going into the bedroom to change her long dress. I hate girls who swear.

'You haven't got a date, have you?' she said, popping her head out of the bedroom, dressed only in her bra and panties. I looked the other way. 'I mean on the Heath. Zak says that's where they all meet. He often goes there, for laughs. Come on, tell me all about it. What do you do?'

She came and bent down in front of me, her breasts drooping onto my chin. The smell of sweat had gone. She had elastic marks just below her belly button and a brown birth mark at the top of her thigh. I could see the top of her pubic hair, in a straight line as it's supposed to be. Blokes' pubic hair comes to a point. That's how you know the difference.

'I want *you* to tell me,' I said. 'How often does Zak go on the Heath, then? Who does he meet?'

I must have been too eager with my questions, pushing things. She suddenly got bored and I could tell I would have to go carefully if I wanted to find out about her, Shug and Zak.

'You are rotten,' she said, pulling herself away and standing up straight and stretching herself. 'Zak never tells me anything about anything.'

'I don't know what you think I know,' I said, all jokey, but she had gone back into the bedroom. 'You've got it all wrong. As you'll find out.' I gave what I thought was a growl, going to the bedroom door to watch her. She was spraying under her arm with a deodorant. I sat down again.

She put on an old mini skirt and a purple T shirt, exactly like mine, and went to prepare the spaghetti. I wandered round the flat, looking for signs of Shug, saying wasn't it lucky for me that she'd got a nosh ready for him. On the mantelpiece was a postcard from Glasgow, showing Salvador Dali's St John on the Cross.

'I get desperate every Saturday night,' she said. 'Zak usually goes out somewhere, but I have to stay in with the kids. I sit at the window seeing all the people going out for good times and I feel about a hundred.'

'I'll give you a good time, don't worry.'

'What?'

I'd already noticed this habit of suddenly switching off. She'd be all animated one minute, very excited and enthusiastic, then it would be as if she'd jumped the points and lost contact with what had been going on.

The spaghetti was great. She'd made the sauce herself, buying the best sirloin steak and mincing it, the way her mother had taught her but the way she could rarely do it as she never had the money. Shuggy had given her the money.

I suddenly felt jealous of Shuggy. I was fed up hearing about him. Even if it turned out to be all a joke, and she was just having me on, I'd begun to fancy her, despite myself. The Spanish and the Algerian had done the trick. If I wasn't sick first, I'd probably make it.

We were sitting together on the couch, surrounded by dirty dishes. I'd offered to clean up, really meaning it as I hate dirty dishes around, but she refused. In the kitchen I'd caught sight of a lot more dishes piled up from previous meals, all spaghetti bolognaise by the look of the remnants. The buttons of her T shirt were undone and she had no bra on. I read somewhere that photographers have a supply of ice cubes when they're doing nude pictures to keep the nipples erect. I wanted to get some from the fridge, but I thought she might think I was rather forward. She put her fingers on the top of my waist band. I had an image of milk coming out of her breasts, torrents of it, soaking me completely, then turning to blood with neither of us being able to stop it.

I got up and switched on the TV. She'd mentioned turning it

on earlier, as a joke. I said I just wanted to see the goals again. She
didn't seem hurt or annoyed. Perhaps she was used to Zak and
Shug changing the subject at a vital moment. I asked if she was
sure Zak was in Newcastle. She said she wasn't sure and she didn't
care. I asked if Shug really was in Glasgow. She didn't care and she
wasn't sure. She'd never heard of Joff. She was lying back, her legs
apart. Perhaps she was pissed. I might as well go. Or get it over
with.

'How about a drink?' she said.

'Shhh,' I said. They were showing George Graham's goal for
Arsenal, the first one which went into the net after a scramble. I
had a suspicion that he hadn't scored. It might even have been an
own goal. She was trying to turn my face towards her, but I pushed
her away.

She went to a cupboard and came back with a faded bottle of
brandy. It was sticky and congealed and contained only enough
for two glasses. I said no, I couldn't. She must keep it for a special
occasion. She said this was special. I agreed. Arsenal didn't win the
double every year. I stood up and joined her.

'Don't be scared,' she said, holding tightly on to me.

'I'm not.'

'You're shitting yourself.'

'It's excitement.'

'I won't eat you. Just a little nibble perhaps.'

'That's what worries me. I don't want to let you down.'

'Don't be daft. Just enjoy yourself. I always do.'

It wasn't a boast, but it wasn't a reassurance either. She started
to take off her skirt and T shirt and went into the bedroom. I sat
down for a few minutes. My head was throbbing and I felt limp
and exhausted as if I'd been on the job all night.

I thought about slipping off, while she was in the bedroom. I
never once worried about Zak arriving home. He was a well-built
bloke. He could have half killed me, if he'd wanted to. I put the
brandy bottle to my lips, swigging the last drops.

She was under a sheet, luckily. I didn't want to look at her
naked. I didn't want her to see me. I stripped with my back to her,
ignoring her giggles.

'You've got a lovely body,' she said. 'Stand still. Let me look.'

'Give over,' I said. 'You're embarrassing me.'

'I love lithe men. I hate them all muscle bound.'

I went to the bathroom, carefully walking so she saw only my back. One of my many fears is of pissing at the wrong moment. The bath was coated in dirty tide marks. On the side of it lay an empty circular tin, covered in fresh talcum powder. Beside it was a tube of cream. On a rack over the bath was a pile of kids' toys, old boats, ducks, empty shampoo bottles from Sainsbury's and an old brown diaphragm which the kids obviously played with. It was much smaller than the pink circular tin. I went limp and felt sick. I couldn't pee, yet I was bursting.

'Hurry up,' she shouted. 'What are you doing in there? Playing with yourself?' Another one accusing me.

'I can't pee with you shouting. Shut the door.'

She started laughing. I managed at last and went slowly into the bedroom, climbing quickly in beside her, pulling the sheet tightly round me, waiting desperately for something to happen, the quicker the better. Nothing happened. The more it didn't hap-pen, the more worried I became. She chattered on, about her kids, about her Mum's house in Alfriston and how they loved going there and what they must have been doing all day. It didn't do any good. And she knew it. At last she moved over me. I burst into tears and held on to her, saying I was sorry, I was sorry. She held me gently, turning on her back, looking at the ceiling and told me not to worry. It was all right. She was sorry as well. It was her fault.

I fell into a daze after that. I don't know what happened, if anything. I felt wet and limp. I might have done. I might not. It was dark and she was sound asleep, one arm over me. I got up, trying not to wake her. She awoke and said no, don't go. Stay till the morning. I didn't have to leave her now. The kids weren't coming home till Sunday afternoon. Please don't go. What had I to go for? She was imploring me.

'I've got to. Sssh. Go back to sleep.'

I pulled my trousers on. I had no reason to go. Nobody was waiting for me. Nobody knew. Nobody cared. I just felt com-pelled. The more she pleaded with me to wait until morning, the more I was determined. I put my jacket on, leaned over her and kissed her, and then I left. I wanted away from it all quickly, to be cleansed and forget it all.

12

I woke up early. I felt very fresh, despite a week of early morning runs. It was becoming a habit. I'd changed my ways and now I was becoming used to it, perhaps even enjoying it, if I didn't watch out. I rang Eddie and got no reply. I wanted to get in touch with Joff. He was at the bottom of most things. Early morning joke.

I had a glass of unsweetened orange juice and changed into my track suit. If I didn't keep fit during the long summer months, I'd never manage the heavy grounds in the winter. There was a possibility we were going to fit in a few matches against other Sunday morning teams. Ginger was to be the captain. I wanted to be one of the ones chosen.

My first job was to take a load of dogs from Pinner to the West End for a theatrical audition. Mr Innocent gave me strict instructions to find out if they got the part and then to offer Fantastic's services in running them to the theatre every night. The woman in charge was a real butch who was kissing and petting them all over. I didn't even help them out of the car, never mind wait and see if they got the job. I didn't want that lot in my car again.

Mr Innocent was wasted in mini-cabs, so I told him when I got back. He needed something where, after his initial genius had been injected, the firm took off on its own and brought him an income for life. Mini-cabs were ridiculous. You were always on the job. He just smiled and said he wasn't doing too bad, not too bad at all, lend us a quid till Monday, eh.

I told him to get knotted. I'd regret it, he told me, going all confidential. He'd been negotiating secretly with three convents to get a contract and at last he was about to get it. His big problem was the right sort of transport. He said our cars would be useless. I said our cars had been good enough so far, doing all his boring London Airports, so what was wrong with them now? The wrong shape, that was the problem, said Mr Innocent. He'd have to get on to Shell or Esso or the Milk Marketing Board. See if they could help.

Then he said he was going to do me this huge favour. I could have the Ayrshire job. He had to stay in London now. I said thanks, but no. I also had to stay in London. He wasn't the only one with things happening. And anyway, I hated going out of town and I hated the North. He said the job would be worth £20, I said no. I wasn't money mad, like him. My pleasure came first. He started sniggering and making remarks about my sort of pleasures. He could tell Sparkle a thing or two. She thought I was such a clean-living bloke, didn't she.

'I saw who you was with on TV the other day,' he said, all sly and leering. 'Holding hands as well. I didn't know you was like that.'

I said I didn't know what he was talking about. He was like a child when he started his clumsy innuendoes, which he thought were so witty. When you didn't get them, he'd go all huffy and say never mind then, never mind.

'It's for you,' said Sparkle, handing me the phone. 'Somebody called Sally.'

'Oh, oh,' said Mr Innocent, slobbering again all over the place. I could have hit him. 'Ask her if she's got her purple dress on, eh.'

He waddled out of the office, his huge arse bursting out of his trousers. They were blue and his jacket, which belonged to another suit, was dark brown, though years of cigarette stain had turned it into a mucky grey. His neck was hanging about three inches over the collar of his drip-dry shirt. It had been white and was now yellow. He refused to wear a vest and his enormous saggy nipples hung down almost to his belly button. Luckily he always wore braces which managed to corset in some of his bulging breasts. Those nuns deserved everything they got if they believed whatever he was telling me. It struck me that he was probably about to illegally import Indian novice nuns. I'd read that all British convents were getting hard up for nuns. If he wanted me to do any nun-running in the middle of the night from Dover harbour, he could think again.

'Yes,' I said, putting my hand over the mouthpiece and telling Sparkle to go and shut the door. I didn't want everyone to hear my business. Sparkle didn't count. It was part of her qualifications, not being able to read, write or count.

Sally sounded very worried. Was she pregnant and about to blame me? That wasn't possible for a start. Since the day of the Cup Final I'd deliberately kept completely away from her street. I'd decided I never wanted to see her again. I was revolted by her almost as much as I'd been revolted by myself.

'Can you come round,' she said. I could hear her shouting in the background to the kids to close the door. She must be in a telephone booth.

All these years I've never got mixed up with anyone like Sally, yet one stupid little night was about to bring me a load of trouble. It's always innocent blokes like me who get caught. People like Joff who are laying everything, married or single, jail bait or geriatric, never get caught. I slip up once and I'm in the shit for ever.

'I'm just going up to Ayrshire,' I said, lying quickly. 'I must rush. I'll be away all week . . .'

'Don't hang up,' she said. 'That couldn't be better . . .'

Another mistake. I'm such a rotten liar. Not only do I mix myself up, I start lies before they are necessary. I should have found out first what she wanted, then lied accordingly. She probably wanted me to go and see Shuggy in Glasgow, find out why he hadn't come back to lay her. I was such a bad stand-in.

She went into a long explanation, throwing addresses at me. I listened carefully and then I said ok, ok, if I had time. She really was very worried. I'd see what I could do. I'm too nice a bloke. That's my trouble.

It was a Russian journalist I had to take to Ayrshire and he turned out to be very interesting. He was football mad and we talked it for most of the way up. He wanted to know my whole life story, not prying, just interested in my views on England, all the jobs I'd done, why I'd changed so often. With a stranger, I felt I could tell him things naturally.

He gave me £30 when I dropped him at Burns' cottage, plus a present of a Russian gramophone record, the original version of Midnight in Moscow, the one the Western jazz bands pinched, so he said.

In the morning, I headed for Newcastle, through lines of deserted pit villages. Everything seemed so small and desolate, most of all the people. Every time I stopped someone and asked the way, I felt a freak. My accent was all wrong, my clothes stood out, even my face and body seemed different from them. I'd been brought up in a council house, just like Zak had been, yet it was as if I'd come from a different planet. No wonder Sally, from her posh Sussex background, had never liked it.

Sally had become very worried about Zak. She'd contacted everyone who might know where he was and they all said they hadn't seen him. It was typical of him to go off somewhere on a whim, but not to disappear for so long without contacting her. She was sure he must be at his mother's. He'd been looking for a job, back up in the North, which she'd said was absolutely daft. She'd sent a letter and a telegram to his mother, but hadn't received an answer.

I knocked at the back door and waited. I tried the latch and it went up. I opened it slightly and shouted hello. Still no reply. I went in, slowly. I could hear a clock ticking in the living room. There was the crackle of a coal fire. It was mid summer, but the house was freezing. I could smell cigarettes and stale tea. I felt someone was watching me. I shouted hello again, louder this time. There was a noise of a chair creaking.

I hadn't noticed him watching me. He was in an old rocking chair, sitting beside the fire, almost obscured by a clothes horse covered with steaming clothes. He was wearing a white shirt with no collar, and carpet slippers. There were ring marks all the way along the arms of the chair where he'd stood his mugs of tea.

'I've come to see Zak,' I said, hurriedly mumbling it, trying to appear honest and a genuine visitor, not a burglar, and at the same time hide my London accent.

His arm moved up stiffly, like a miniature crane in a seaside fun-fair, and he banged a mug of tea down on the arm rest, loudly and squarely, but luckily. He smiled at me, triumphantly, his lips curling. I'd doubted that he'd been capable of doing it. Well he'd done it. But his hand suddenly jerked again, by itself, without him wanting it to, and the mug was sent flying across the floor, breaking into pieces, thick tea splattering like brown seaweed on the floor.

I rushed to help but he pushed me away. I stood helplessly watching as he spluttered and choked and cursed. He got himself straight in the chair again, wiped his mouth with a rag, and started rocking backwards and forwards, looking at me. I wished I'd changed. Put something old and anonymous on. Bright colours, even on a cheap T shirt, were out of place.

'Where's Zak?' I asked.

'He doesn't live here no more.'

'I know. Where is he?'

'He lives in London.'

'I know.'

'Are you his friend?'

It was a statement, not a question. He looked me carefully up and down. Just the sort of friend Zak would have. He'd told him he'd end up with a friend like me. He should never have gone to London.

On the mantelpiece was a line of photographs, all of Zak in very prissy-looking poses, naked on a rug with a dog, in a sailor suit with his hair slicked down, right up to a synthetic colour photo of him in his academic dress of mortar board and gown, receiving his degree. His complexion was limpid white. The photographer must have gone to a lot of trouble to clean out Zak's spots.

I asked again if Zak had been home and he shouted at me this time that he lived in London. I wasn't making myself clear, or he was deliberately being unhelpful. Instead I asked if Zak was an only child. I knew nothing about him, now that I stared round at all the signs of his early life. He was a mistake, said the old man. He'd never wanted him. They had three lasses and they were just getting them off their hands when Zak came along, fifteen years younger than the girls. It was all her fault. I asked why there were no pictures of his daughters. He said She wouldn't allow them. He was hers, anyway. She's made him what he was.

'When did you see him last?' I asked.

'I never see him,' he said.

'What time is your wife in?'

'I never see her. I see nobody. Who are you anyway?'

I got up and went to the kitchen to make him some more tea. If I'd smoked I could have given him a cigarette. Then he might have told me something. I had a proper look round the kitchen. On a shelf in the pantry I found a telegram from Sally lying on top of a tin of baked beans where it had been torn open, read and left. She'd signed it from Sally, Tom, Ben and Nathalie. She'd dragged the kids into it. Perhaps she'd thought they wouldn't know her, or care, if she just signed it Sally. On the top shelf, lying in a corner, was a letter from Zak. I put it in my pocket.

'He's looking for a job up here,' I said, giving him the tea.

'Who?'

'Zak is.'

'Stupid booger.'

He clammed up again, now I'd brought Zak back into the conversation. I asked if he thought United should have sold Pop Robson to West Ham. I hit a chord and we were away, going backwards at a great pace. That was another thing he disliked about Zak. He was never interested in football. I told him things had changed. Zak was now a dead keen player, but he wasn't listening. He'd got on to Jacky Milburn. I hadn't noticed that a woman in an off-white raincoat, with short bleached hair, had arrived home. She dumped her bags on the table and stood in front of me, waiting for me to explain. She looked about fifty and I presumed it must be Zak's mother. It turned out to be one of his sisters. She stood, arms a-kimbo, accusingly, hating me, wanting me out, just when I'd broken down the old man. Zak definitely hadn't been home for six months, she said. She had no idea where he was. She didn't care.

'Well, fine, thanks,' I said, moving to the door. 'Sorry to bother you.'

She came with me to the gate, seeing me off the premises, off the edge of the world if she could manage it.

'Why do you want him anyway?'

'I was just passing. Thought I'd look him up.'

'What's wrong with him?'

'Nothing, nothing.'

She watched me get into the car then she came out of the gate, holding the car door open, stopping me driving away. She suddenly had gone from being simply nasty and suspicious to being worried and frightened.

'There must be something wrong. You wouldn't come all this way.'

'Really, I was just passing,' I said. 'He'll be all right.'

'What do you mean? Where is he? Why shouldn't he be all right?'

I hadn't been thinking what I was saying, but I only made it worse by trying to explain what I'd meant, when I didn't know what I'd meant.

'Are you the queer he's been getting money from?'

She looked me up and down and I thought she was going to spit at me. I wanted to push her out of the way, slam the door shut and go, but this time I wanted to know what she meant.

'You what?' I said. 'Who told you all that?'

'We know. He wasn't like that up here, you know. It's London that's done it, and her.'

I'd never thought that Zak was bent. Not just because of his wife and kids and all that, which proves nothing, but because I'd never sensed it. You usually can. It's an awareness, a preening, which gives it away.

She then launched into an attack on Sally, calling her a slut and a bitch and sex mad. She'd make anyone queer, the way she pawed Zak, all over him, disgusting, and any other man she could get her hands on. She'd seen it herself. They'd all warned Zak. But they didn't know it would end up like this. He'd better not come back here, that was all.

I asked again how she knew. She must have got it all wrong. What was this queer like, the one who was supposed to be paying him? But all she wanted to do was attack Sally.

There was a loud shout from the house and a series of crashes. Her father must have fallen off his rocking chair. As she turned to look in the direction of the house, I pushed her aside, slammed the door shut and drove off.

I kept my head down for about a hundred miles on the A1, keeping up a steady 70 miles an hour. There seemed to be a lot of police around, but it was probably my imagination. On the Doncaster By-pass there had been a three-car smash, with at least one dead. It must just have happened. The body was still on the side of the road, covered in a blanket.

I stopped in a lay-by and got out Zak's letter. There were HP sauce stains all over it, covering many of the words. It was just a bread-and-butter letter, with the sauce as extra, saying he was sorry he wasn't coming after all. There was a paragraph about things going wild at home, or it might have been well, but it got lost in the sauce. There were only three paragraphs. The last one was about the kids and their latest sayings. It was a boring note. I screwed it up and threw it in the car ash tray, along with my Polos, my paper clips, the spare key and other necessities of life.

It was about eight o'clock when I hit London. I came in with no trouble, having missed all the home-going traffic. I felt I'd been away for weeks, not just two days and a night. I felt the fashions had changed, people had died, world-shattering events had happened and I'd never know about them and never catch up.

But I felt I'd caught up with Zak, in a way. Three sisters and a doting Mum and a daft Dad. I could see where a lot of it came from. But it was still surprising news, that they thought he was queer. If you're on the dole, of course, there's not much you can sell, except your body.

13

I thought about Zak all next day at work. I spent the morning driving round in a dream, trying to recall all the bits and pieces about him. At lunch time I rang Sally, which I'd been putting off doing, hoping it would go away. I knew I should, otherwise she would come and see me. That was the last thing I wanted.

The people in the flat next door to Sally had a phone and I rang her there, knowing it would be difficult to get involved when there were other people around. I told her simply that Zak wasn't at Newcastle, they hadn't seen him, but they were sure he was ok.

Sally said she wasn't sure at all. In fact now she was more worried than ever. If she hadn't heard from him by this evening, she was going to the police. She was also broke. I offered to lend her something, if she was really desperate. I knew her parents were loaded, so I didn't push it too far. She said she'd manage, somehow.

It suddenly struck me it was Wednesday, Zak's signing-on day. Wherever he was, he must be broke as well. Surely he would be turning up for his free money, something he didn't have to sell anything to get.

I told Mr Innocent I was taking the afternoon off. I'd done two days out of town so I deserved the break. I went home first to pick up my football pads and training shoes. I might be trying to help a friend but there was no reason not to enjoy myself as well.

I'd never seen Zak completely naked, now I thought about it, though he was one of those real show-offs who always changed on the side of the pitch. Even when I played football as a kid, wearing two pairs of shorts in case one had to come off, I was very conscious of displaying myself in public. In private, that's a different matter.

He was well endowed, as I'd seen. I always seem to be smaller than anyone else. They all look like donkeys and put me to shame. I was once in a pub in Kentish Town and I went to the lav at the same time as the pianist in the group. He was a little bloke, almost a dwarf, but I've never seen anyone as big. It took him both hands to control it, and he had equally big hands. It went on for ages. I just couldn't perform, or avert my eyes. He was whistling away, nodding his head, unconcerned, probably used to people watching him. He wasn't showing off. He probably thought he was normal. He gave me a great inferiority complex for years. I was about eighteen at the time. It was more than its size which worried me. It was my fascination with its existence which troubled me. I couldn't take my eyes off it.

I usually looked away when Zak was stripping off. I thought it was a bit much anyway, when we still had a few ten-year-olds playing with us, though over the months we'd got rid of the youngest and most useless kids. Now we had two good teams, eleven a side, and everyone had football boots, pads and proper gear. Recently

Zak had got a red jock strap and was always telling everyone to go down to Camden Town and get one. Perhaps after the dole, I might just pop in. Why deprive myself any longer?

The Labour Exchange looked very posh and impressive from outside, like someone's town house. I parked at the front and looked round for the right door to go in. There were lots of entrances, marked C, D, A and B, and I couldn't decide.

'I'm an investigator from the SS,' said a deep voice behind me. 'I've come to arrest you.'

It was Mr Innocent. I'd been surprised, rather than frightened, but I must have looked pretty alarmed. He leaned against the wall, paralysed at his own wit, his huge belly going up and down. Then suddenly he went serious and clutched his heart.

'Quick, quick, my pills,' he said, his hands trembling. I couldn't decide whether he was putting it on, but I searched in his trouser pockets, through all the dirt and fluff and unpaid bills, looking for his little silver pill box. I don't know why he kept it in there. He always found it an effort putting his hands in his trouser pockets, even when he wasn't dying of a coronary. It was a real silver pill box, an antique snuff box, with the initials J B on it. He maintained J B had been an uncle, but I didn't believe him. His flesh felt creepy. The lining of his pocket was all matted and dirty. He seemed to have no underpants on, by the feel of him. It was as if he was dead, taking such liberties with all that strange flesh.

I found the box at last and took out seven pills, all different colours. These were seven he was supposed to take five times a day, when he remembered. They were mostly for his angina. He swallowed them and eventually stopped panting. He hadn't been putting it on, but I think it was a false alarm. He'd been laughing so much he'd started to choke and had imagined it was an attack.

A huge queue had begun to form round us, a long line of apathetic faces stretching from the paying-out entrance right round the building. It was almost two o'clock, time for the afternoon session to begin. They had all stood to one side as I'd helped Mr Innocent with his imagined heart attack. Not interested. Just moving out of our way.

He was soon laughing and joking again. I said I was surprised to see him. I hadn't seen his car at the front. He put his fingers to his lips and winced theatrically. I hadn't to give away that he worked. The SS had spies in every queue. He said he always left his car several streets away. Always? Of course. He'd been collecting unemployment benefit for years. And sick pay. He did have a dodgy ticker, didn't he? If I split on him, he'd split on me. He was all conspiratorial. Mates together, laughing and slapping my back.

For some reason, I didn't want to tell him the reason I was at the dole. It was just a hunch anyway. I didn't want Mr Innocent to get his nose into Zak and Sally's affairs. What was I going to say to Zak anyway? Come home, all is forgiven? He'd probably left her for ever. I'd be told not to interfere. Or simply get thumped.

Mr Innocent was asking me when my signing-on time was. He said his was 2 o'clock. I said mine was 2.30. He said he was surprised we hadn't met in the queue before. What a joke. Both working for Fantastic and both conning the SS. He turned round to the queue and pretended to kill them all with a tommy gun, rat tat tat. Then he had to pause for breath. He was exhausting himself again. Nobody had taken any notice of him. I wanted to ask him what SS meant but it would show my ignorance, either of the dole queue or his infantile jokes.

As we were talking, a nun came down the queue, giving out leaflets. Mr Innocent started edging away from me, going all coy and nervous, prodding me in the ribs. I recognised the nun, although I wouldn't have done so if he hadn't drawn my attention to her. It was Sister Mary, one of our regular customers. Mr Innocent took her from her convent in Highgate to one near the Balls Pond Road every Thursday afternoon. He wouldn't tell us why. Midge maintained they were having it off.

'You're all right then Michael, are you, all right,' said Mr Innocent, getting himself even more confused as he tried an Irish accent and a little tap dance. 'Do be careful, will you.' He had his arm round my shoulder. As the sister approached, he gave me a last friendly hug and began to move away.

'I'll be off then for my passport,' he said, waving a card he'd taken from his pocket. 'Oh hello, Sister. What a pleasure to see you.' And he disappeared into an entrance further along the queue marked C. When I got near to it, I could see that it did say Passports. But there was no sign of Mr Innocent.

There was a sudden move forward at two o'clock when the entrance opened. We jerked forward in fits and starts. I kept my eye on people joining the queue behind me but I could see nobody I knew. Inside the queue split into about five little queues, all winding round a large corridor, ending up at five different boxes along a long counter. One counter seemed to consist of doss house down-and-outs, all bearded and tattered.

A couple of hippie types just inside the door were giving out leaflets. It was a duplicated sheet about the Claimants Union. There was a quotation from Marx and then a list of the atrocities committed by the investigators from the Social Security. So that was what it meant.

Zak's signing-on time was 2.30. He'd told me many a time that he was never late. You couldn't afford to be. You'd lose your money if you were. By three o'clock there was still no sign of him. He couldn't have been early, as I'd been there before it opened. I was sure I hadn't missed him, unless he'd slipped in and out while I'd been messing around with Mr Innocent. Everyone was very orderly, patiently waiting their turn, so he couldn't have jumped the queue. I got to the top of the queue about four times, and then stepped aside, pretending to examine one of the lists of job vacancies. I'd begun to feel one of them, as deprived and humiliated as the rest. Zak had told me how he hated it. Everyone there was to some extent a failure. There was no point in romanticising it. At first, you argued and shouted and refused to get beaten, but eventually you went along with it all, shuffling the weeks, the months, your life away.

I gave up at 3.30. My legs were stiff with standing. As a last check, I went up some stairs I hadn't noticed before. I came to another waiting room, this time full of little confessional boxes, all of them occupied, with people being put through it, describing the dreadful sins they'd committed by becoming unemployed. It was obviously the place the newcomers checked in at. Out of the first box came Ginger, an inane but rather dazed smile on his face.

We walked out together. He went all aggressive the minute we got outside, saying what a joke, he was going to con those bastards out of £3 a week, but I could tell he'd been affected by the grilling. I asked him if he fancied a game of football. I was going for one myself. He had to go home first to change his good shoes. He'd put them on specially for the interview. I said I'd drive him home.

He lived in a brand new block of high-rise council flats, not far behind Kentish Town High Road. I'd heard about them, as they were supposed to be show houses, architect designed and all that, but I'd never been there. I told Ginger I remembered the area when it used to be old terrace houses and I'd gone this way for a Marine Ice. He looked at me as if I'd come out of the Ark.

His father was in, which I hadn't expected. He'd just got out of bed, having been on the night shift. He stared at me suspiciously. I did look a bit old to be one of Ginger's mates and a bit different. I explained that I played football with Ginger, which puzzled him even more. Ginger left me and went off into another room. He hadn't even introduced me. Just left me to hang about.

I admired the view and the lovely flat, which it was. I told him I remembered the estate when it was terrace houses, going for a Marine Ice. He remembered it as well. Those were the good days. He wished they'd never built these new blocks. You met the wrong type. They just put anyone in them. Now in the old terrace houses, you knew everyone. Everyone was friendly, helped everyone. Not like this block. There was nothing for the kids to do, except get into trouble. Not of course that his lad ever got into trouble. He got up and brought out a pile of glossy colour prints of Ginger as a little boy, of Ginger's drawings, Ginger's little poems. What a good boy he'd been. No trouble at all.

He asked me if I'd like a cup of tea. I said yes, then I duly admired Ginger receiving his Duke of Edinburgh's Award, his bronze.

'He was forever over the Fields as a kid, picking flowers, birds' eggs, the lot. You name it, he knew it. I wanted him to go on to university and be a doctor, but you know how it is with these young lads. They want to leave with all their mates and make money. I blame his mates really, for encouraging him.'

His Dad had very close-cropped hair and a big leather belt and very intense eyes. His forearms were covered in tattoos, all telling of his love for Lilly. He'd got Ginger his job as an apprentice electrician, a very good job to have got. He'd pulled a few strings, rung a few mates, and got him taken on. No son of his was going to be a labourer. Ginger had obviously not yet told his Dad he was on the dole.

He was very pleased that Ginger was studying for his Higher National, two evenings a week at the Tech. He wouldn't be an electrician for long. Saturday night was the only night he was allowed out, although his so-called friends were always calling for him, trying to stop him studying. He was very pleased he'd taken up football again. He could have been a professional, if he'd put his mind to it. He hoped I'd organise a few more games. I said I'd do my best.

Ginger came back, and groaned when he saw what his Dad had got out. He groaned even more when his Dad triumphantly pulled out one of him as a choir boy, in his surplice and ruff. When the letter from Blue Peter was brought out, thanking him for sending in the lovely bottle tops, Ginger said he was going. He couldn't stand it any more. His Dad put all the stuff away, sighing, and poured me out another cup of tea.

The flat was immaculate, everything new and bright and modern, with a big TV, stereo, central heating, balconies, and a set of Arthur Mee's children's encyclopaedias, brand new and untouched. I asked where his Mum was and was told she was at work. I thought of Zak's council house in Newcastle, circa 1936, which was like a slum by comparison.

'After football, we're going to the Club, aren't we, Franko?' said Ginger, making faces at me. 'It's a discussion tonight. Franko's speaking, ain't you. I've got to go and listen to my mate, haven't I.'

His Dad said that was news to him. His mother had given him strict instructions that he had to have his Tech work done for tomorrow. She hadn't mentioned no youth club.

'He won't be late,' I said. 'We have tea and buns at 9.30, and that's it. Ready, Ginger? Better put a tie on, don't you think.'

It took me back to my teenage days, helping your mates to get out. His Dad was still very worried, but he made no more objections. Ginger said he'd be back at 9.30, bags of time to do his Tech work before he went to bed.

I wondered where we would go. A pub probably. I had at last become his friend so now I'd get into their gang properly and jump the generation gap and see what it was like. I hoped he wasn't going dancing or chasing girls. I'd be forced to go along as well and pretend I was interested. The girls all had short hair and looked more like the boys than the boys did, with equally big boots and dark coats.

We went down in the lift with Ginger pushing his hair back, arranging it neatly. He got out some cigarettes and lit up. He didn't offer me one, which I wanted him to, even though I don't smoke. Perhaps he knew already.

We walked across the estate together, past the arty-crafty statues of twisted mothers and children, done in white concrete, now covered with red paint and slogans. We walked across the grass, ignoring a notice telling us not to, and through someone's back yard, over a fence, across a balcony, taking short cuts all the time. It was a new way to the Heath I didn't know. I asked him what he was going to do this evening. Dunno, he said.

I remembered how exciting it used to be. The night always started off boringly, a game on the Heath and you genuinely didn't know where you were going next. Time seemed to hang so heavily, but once the lads got out and got together, something usually turned up, like football under the lampposts or going up West to look at the crowds, or going into someone's house to listen to Guy Mitchell records.

Ginger had his best Dr Martin boots on, very highly polished and gleaming. There was about a two-inch gap above them where his trousers ended and the boots began. I made a note to be on his side. His body was slightly arched and he walked leaning forward, his hair falling over his face.

We got to the main road. He turned sharply and said, See you. It was so quick, I felt sure I hadn't heard him properly.

'See you,' he said again, stopping, looking at me, refusing to move any further until I went away.

'I thought we were going to play football,' I said, smiling at him.

'You thought wrong.'

'What are you going to do then?'

'Dunno.'

'Oh,' I said, slowly. 'In that case, see you . . .' I began to move away, still not sure I'd got it right.

'Ginger,' I called after him. 'You won't forget what your Dad said, will you . . .'

'Piss off,' he said.

He turned round and walked quickly up the street, his boots clumping on the pavement, too big for his thin legs, too big for his body.

I bought an *Evening Standard*, to give myself something to do, although I always prefer to buy the last edition. I couldn't face football now. I just wanted to go home, to creep away, out of sight.

I made some coffee, although I knew Gran would say that was spoiling my evening meal. What was the point of her slaving over a hot porridge if I had filled myself up with nasty instant coffee. I had some chocolate biscuits, just to compound the crime, and a piece of Dundee cake. Fat people are supposed to retreat to the fridge for solace when they've got problems, which makes them fatter. I didn't care about getting fat. I was too depressed. Just as I finished the Dundee cake off Gran arrived. She moaned and groaned on about me eating before a meal. I got out the *Evening Standard* and got behind it so I didn't have to listen to her.

Zak was on the front page. There was a very blurry picture of him, cut out of a family snapshot, which they'd managed to spread across three columns. His body had been identified at lunch time by his wife. The police had been searching for clues since his naked body was found, battered to death, three weeks ago on a corner of Hampstead Heath frequented by lovers. The report didn't say what kind of lovers, but made it clear by saying there had been a spate of attacks on single men in the same corner all summer. The fact that Zak was married with kids rather spoiled their innuendoes, but they were sticking to them all the same. I could see where Sally and the kids had been cut out of the photograph.

I began to feel shivery. Gran was in the kitchen, still moaning. I didn't want her to know. I felt guilty and shaken. Zak was the first dead person in my life I'd known personally. I thought about ringing Sally. It was the least I could do. Her worries about Zak had proved right.

All her friends would probably be contacting her and rushing round. She wouldn't want anyone else. If she'd identified the body, the police would probably still be with her, questioning her about Zak's friends. I wondered if she'd told them about me. I wasn't such a close friend of Zak's really. Just a footballing friend, nothing intimate. I knew Sally better. I'd only slept with her, after all. Christ, I must have been raving.

14

I had an early telephone call, to get me up for a seven o'clock job to Gatwick. Afterwards I went into the office, put the phone on the answering system, and tried to write a letter to Sally. I was going to be so busy all that day that I'd convinced myself I wouldn't have the time to go and see her. I'd also convinced myself that everyone would be ringing her, or at least her neighbour, and she wouldn't want to be bothered by me on the phone.

Sparkle was in the caff next door where I'd sent her. I could see her with her cup of tea balanced against her cheek, lost in some deep sexual fantasy. Out of the corner of his mouth, Midge had told me he fancied her. Could I find out, as I was so close to her, if she fancied him. If I'd been Mr Innocent, I would really have stirred it up and have had them into bed together at once, probably in the front window, with the whole street watching. What better advert for Fantastic's speed? Over the front door hung Mr Innocent's latest home-made motto: Fantastic do it Faster. Every week he put up a new slogan. He'd got the idea from a butcher's shop in Camden Town which puts up allegedly funny notices every day.

'Dear Sally, if there is anything I can do, please let me know.' Then I got stuck. Perhaps I should begin with some well-chosen words about her bereavement. Gran was always good at saying the right things. Or make a joke. Or I could tell her more about Newcastle and what his Dad had said and his sister. No, I wouldn't tell her what his sister had said. As Zak was now dead, there wasn't much point in saying anything else about Newcastle. After all, I only wanted to offer help, as remotely as possible, without getting involved again. I signed it Luv, Franko. Love might have looked too serious, and that was the last thing I wanted. Luv made it a bit jokey. I wrote it on Fantastic notepaper and put it in the basket for Sparkle to post. I might as well send it free. The thought struck me that Joff had done the same, on BBC notepaper to Eddie. I was about to tear it up when Mr Innocent drew up, not in his car, but in an ancient van which said Bulk Liquid. He was looking very pleased with himself.

'What do you think then, Franko?'

'How many nuns are you going to get in there?'

'I mean about Zak,' said Mr Innocent, rubbing his great beefy hands together. 'I always expected it you know. Clever bugger. Thought he was it. But his wife's ok. A real goer, isn't she, Franko?'

'Get stuffed,' I said.

'Yes please, darling.'

He went off, waddling down the office, his shoulders trembling at his own wit.

'Sparkle gone for me tea then, has she?'

At that moment Sparkle came back, with a paper cup of tea for Mr Innocent, but none for me I noticed. She and Mr Innocent started swapping boring non-stories about Zak, what they'd thought of him, how awful he'd been, what a know-all, and it was about time the police cleared up those woods. I think neither had ever spoken to him more than once.

I went across to the caff where I was joined by Midge. I told him Sparkle did fancy him but Mr Innocent of all people was trying to lay her so he'd better get in there first. Midge looked very dejected. It had happened again. In all their years together, they always fancied Mr Innocent but never him. I said he must be joking. No one could fancy that slob. He said I'd be surprised. Lots of girls found him very sexy.

Back in the office, Sparkle and Mr Innocent were still at it, huddled together in a corner, whispering at each other. All they could do was run Zak down. Nobody had any sympathy for Sally, left with three young kids to bring up. They didn't consider it a tragedy at all. In her own way, Sally had loved him. But they didn't care. It was just another source of gossip, till the next one came along. The phone rang and I made great show of answering it myself, telling Sparkle loudly just to sit still, she was far too busy to do any work, I'd look after it. Someone wanted a car to take a pile of books to the London Library. I said I'd do it.

I put the job in the book, just for the record, and slammed out of the office. In the car I realised that the basket next to the order book was empty. My letter had gone. Sparkle couldn't have posted it already. I would have seen her from the caff if she'd gone out. Perhaps she'd put it in her handbag to post later.

I planned to finish early, about four o'clock, as I'd been on since seven o'clock. Mr Innocent always tried to get me to work longer. He couldn't understand anyone only doing an eight-hour day when he never did less than twelve himself. I was turning away money. I was quite happy with what I had. I wasn't greedy, like some people. The point of being a mini-cab driver was the freedom and independence. If I became a slave to putting in the hours and chalking up the pounds, I might as well go back to the old days.

I could see him waiting for me when I came in for my last job, his belly up against the window, his finger up his nose. If that was sexy I'd rather have Midge. I brushed him aside, saying no, I definitely couldn't do any more jobs. After this last one, I was going for a run. He was waving the *Evening Standard* at me, asking if I'd read it. I took no notice of him and went straight out again.

I wasn't actually going for a run. I was going to play football. I had an old shirt on, knowing I'd be pouring out pints of sweat, and under my long trousers I had shin pads on. Gran always worried, like Grans of all ages and sexes, about being knocked down in dirty underwear. I wonder what people would think if I was in a crash and I was found to be wearing shin pads for driving. Mr Innocent once had an old lady who lived in the Holly Lodge estate who wore a crash helmet every time he drove her anywhere. She'd crouch in the back, terrified. Mr Innocent always drove more like an idiot than usual, just to make her more frightened. He went to pick her up one day and found her in her back garden, dead. She'd been sitting alone in her huge lawns, absolutely peaceful, miles from any nasty traffic, and a bee had stung her. It was one of Mr Innocent's best horror stories. He never failed to get a laugh.

I went on the Heath and found Ginger and the rest of the lads playing on the usual spot, near the running track. I joined in, like any other evening, but deliberately didn't say anything to Ginger. I wanted to show him I was above any petty behaviour. After we'd finished he was the one who started talking, all matey, asking if I was coming for a drink. I said no, but not nastily. I enjoyed playing football with him. There was no excitement when he wasn't there. There was a tension around when Ginger was there, playing football or just messing about. You didn't know what he was going to do next. I said, see you, got to get home.

I had a shower, shampooed my hair and settled down with a glass of beer and a packet of crisps, though I wondered about the crisps. Playing football was keeping my weight down—I'd lost a stone in six months—but things like crisps would put it all back on again. I should have gone to the pub with them. They didn't eat crisps. Only women ate crisps, Vince, Ginger's mate, had told me.

I thought about peeling the potatoes for Gran coming in. I knew she'd told me to do something, but I couldn't remember whether she'd said it was chips or curry this evening. She wouldn't mind. She didn't care for me trying to cook. That was a job for women. But it's funny I've never tried to. People have often been surprised I can't cook. Luckily, everyone I've ever lived with has done the cooking, from Gran to Johnny. Despite all his faults, Johnny was a fantastic cook. I wondered who he was cooking for now.

There was a knock at the door. It opened before I could say anything. In came a very smooth-looking bloke in a dark suit with thick sideboards. He shook my hand, beaming at me, and said he was a policeman. I offered him a crisp but he said he didn't eat crisps on duty, but he would take a beer. I said that was the last bottle, but he could have a drink out of my glass, if he really was a policeman.

I don't know how he'd opened the door. I was sure I'd closed it. Though perhaps on thinking about it, I'd put the snib up, so Gran could get in without ringing. He smiled again, indulging me, and showed me his police card. It might have been his Puffin Club card for all I knew.

I shared the beer out and he sat down, staring round the room. He reminded me of that Russian I took to Scotland. He'd looked completely un-Russian. This un-policeman had long hair, as long as mine anyway, and wet-look shoes. He looked as if he should be running a boutique. The only thing not quite right was his shirt. It was button down. Very last year.

'Reading about yourself, are you?' he said, lighting a cigarette.

I picked up the paper and turned over the pages slowly, finding nothing. He let me carry on, smiling. It was like a game. He was egging me on to the next move. I knew from his expression there was another move to be made. I turned the back page on its side, very studiously reading everything, just to spin it out so he'd be forced to tell me what he wanted, as if I didn't know. There was a paragraph in the stop press, all smudgy as if it had been done with a John Bull printing set. It was in that curious stop press language, all staccato and not enough verbs. Heath murder: police desperate trace mini-cab driver seen taking murdered man Kenwood.

'No photograph,' I said. 'Curses.'

'We're working on that,' he said. 'Have you got an agent?' You could see he thought he was a wit by the size of his own smile.

I asked him how he'd got on to me so quickly, as it had taken them ten days in the first place to identify the body. He said they'd been given information. Could I very carefully go over every detail of what happened that evening. He got out his notebook, which put me off immediately. I wanted to see what he was writing down, whether I spoke grammatically or not. He'd already written two pages.

'No shorthand?' I said.

'Sorry,' he said. 'French, German and Latin. But no shorthand. What time did you pick up Zak and his family . . . ?'

I could remember everything, such as it was. I even got their seating arrangement in the back seat, where Sally had been in relation to the kids, what each of them had been wearing and what they'd all got to eat on their picnic.

I was enjoying it. I've never once been used for a market research test, though I've often hung around Hampstead Tube station when I've seen people being stopped and their opinions solemnly written down on boards.

'What sort of mood would you say they were in? Were they arguing?'

I described the argument over the kids starting to eat in the car instead of waiting for the picnic. How each blamed the other for the kids' disobedience, especially Sally, shouting at Zak that *he* was their father. The policeman wrote it all out very intently. I said perhaps I'd overdone that row. It had been just a normal family thing, not important, not serious or nasty, perhaps he should play it down a bit in his report. He said it wasn't a report. It was just notes, really for his own benefit.

'After he went for his run, did you stay long with his wife?'

'I didn't stay at all.'

'I thought you said you did.' He went through his notes again, turning back the pages.

'Perhaps for a few minutes. That's right. I helped her with the pram and the stuff across the grass to a picnic spot, then I left them. I had other jobs to do. Do you want to hear what the other jobs were?'

He paused. I knew he wanted more about Zak and Sally but I'd honestly told him everything. Just to bore him to death, I went over every detail of the four Burmese gentlemen I'd taken to Windsor. He eventually cut me short, so I didn't have to tell him about the other three people I'd taken to the Heath that night. I was hoarse with talking. Perhaps I wouldn't like being market-researched.

Once more, he wanted me to remember what Zak had been like when he ran off, what sort of mood he was in. I told him again, just a normal sort of mood for him. A bit grumpy with the kids, dying to get off on his run. He was a slave for exercise.

'White plimsolls he was wearing was he?' he said, looking at his notes.

'No, blue ones. At least they'd been painted blue, but the paint might have come off in the water.'

'How do you know he was wearing the plimsolls in the water?'

'Oh that's right,' I said, remembering. 'He was naked of course.'

'How do you know? The newspapers didn't say that.'

'I saw the body coming out. I just happened to be passing.'

'Just happened to be passing. What a coincidence.'

'Wasn't it.'

I paused, waiting for him. He stretched himself, very pleased. Then he leaned forward.

'Why didn't you come and tell us then, if you saw the body?'

'I didn't know it was Zak. His head was covered.'

'But you saw the body, you say. Didn't you recognise that?'

'Funnily enough, I didn't.'

'Very funny,' he said, closing his book. 'Hilarious.'

Still with his book closed, he asked me to remember exactly what I did the rest of that evening. I could tell that he was committing every word to memory, even though he'd closed his book, to fool me into thinking it was now just idle chat.

'I did about two or three other jobs. After the last one, I went home, changed and had a run.'

'Another coincidence. Just like Zak had done.'

'We play in the same football team. Well, a knockabout-side.'

'What time did you finish?'

'I don't know. Perhaps about eight. I came home and went for a run. I'd bought a new track suit. Would you like to see it?'

'I'll save that pleasure for another time. Then what did you do?'

'I watched television and went to bed.'

'Alone?'

'With my Gran.'

'What did you watch?'

'Match of the Day. Or is it the Big Match. Whatever the Saturday night football is called.'

'With your Gran?'

'No, she went to bed at ten.'

'So you sat up alone, watching football. Hmm. Without going out again? I see. And then went to bed. That's great, fine, super. Sorry to have put you through all this. You never know what's going to come up, so you have to go through all the angles, though I know it's a drag. Have yourself another beer.'

'You've forgotten. You helped me finish the last one.'

'Of course,' he said, standing up and stretching himself, as if he'd been doing all the thinking not me. He was all blasé now, another draggy job almost over. 'Nice place you've got here. Must be expensive.'

'Quite,' I said.

'Shall I tell you the most amazing coincidence about this job,' he said, sitting down again. I wanted to get rid of him. Gran would be home any minute and want to know what had been going on.

'Amaze me.'

'I was at university with Zak. Isn't that fantastic?'

'It is rather,' I said. I'm a sucker for coincidences as well, though he was overdoing it, beaming like an idiot, wanting me to applaud.

'Different college, and I didn't really know him. But we both went for jobs at the same time, before the University Appointments Board. Fat lot of good they were. We both tried to join Shell as graduate trainees. Zak got offered a job and I didn't. I tried the police instead.'

'Bad luck.'

'Oh I don't know. Not such a bad old life. You have to be careful though. They're a bit suspicious of graduates. Where did you go?'

'A secondary modern, just down the road.'

I suppose over the years, having mixed with all sorts, I've picked up a passing smoothness. He was a big-headed bloke, but he seemed nice enough. Just doing his job after all. He was still smiling at me, nodding his head. I watched him, overdoing it again, and it struck me that he didn't think for one moment I'd gone to a university. He was trying it on. Buttering me up. The bastard. I stood up, showing I wanted him to go. He got up, thanked me profusely for the drink.

'You know, it's the first time since I transferred to London five years ago that I've come across someone I knew from Durham. You meet Oxford graduates and Cambridge bods everywhere, in all the top jobs. Never anyone from Durham.'

'Proves something,' I said. The way he'd said 'bods' gave him away. That long hair and those sideboards were a real come-on. He was just another middle-class phoney. I could just see him off duty, wearing a coloured Tootal neckerchief over his Double Two shirt. I bet Zak had hated him. Good job he wasn't here.

He'd only been gone ten minutes when Gran arrived. She had a long tale of woe about the rain and the Tube being hours late and why hadn't I been there to meet her. The last thing she'd said was that if it rained I had on no account to meet her at the Tube, I had work to do. This meant if it rained I had to drop everything and be there. She would have moaned either way, being there or not being there, so I just let her prattle on.

'Who's been smoking?' she said, sniffing round, examining my jacket, putting it to her nose. She could always tell when I'd had passengers who smoked, just by sniffing me when I came in.

'Mr Innocent,' I said. 'He was round earlier. I'll make you some tea.'

'I hate your tea. Sit yourself still. You'll be wanting some porridge I suppose.'

I wanted to tell her about Zak, because there was nothing to hide about it, but it was too late and I was too tired. I decided to leave it for the morning. She'd have mentioned it yesterday if she'd seen it in the paper. She obviously hadn't. It was just a little local story after all. What's another body? The newspapers are full of them.

15

When I went to get my car the next morning, it was open. The lock hadn't been forced. I thought at first some yobs had been tampering with it. But there was nothing broken or taken. I must have forgotten to lock it. Every night Gran asks me before bed if I've locked my car. I always say yes, whether I have or not. I was becoming very careless.

Mr Innocent wasn't in the office. Sparkle said he'd gone round to my flat to get me. I groaned. I'd left Gran at home which meant he'd get in. When Mr Innocent came back he said that Mr Howard wanted me urgently. He'd rung first thing. I had to go round there right away. He was all winks and nudges, saying he hoped I had a good time. I was beginning to go right off Mr Innocent.

Joff embraced me when I arrived, stinking of aftershave, and continued squeezing me as he led me into the living room. I hate being touched by compulsive, repulsive touchers like Joff. I hoped Eddie wasn't watching. I didn't want him to think I fancied Joff. There was a lovely smell of fresh coffee and he pressed me to have a glass of whisky as well, even though it was so early in the day.

'Are you free for lunch?' he said.

'I'm working, ain't I?' I was deliberately being gruff and common, just to counter all his smarm.

'I've got a little proposition I want to put to you. Have you been to the Trat?'

'No. I go to Joe's caff.'

'Don't worry. It's all on expenses. Not my bloody money. I'm preparing a programme on taxis and the war with mini-cabs. I think you'd be a natural. Perfect. You look good. Talk good. Gold dust, as far as the box is concerned.'

'The war's over.'

'But I've got some new angles. Things are moving again in the taxi field. All those abortion trips at London Airport. We're going to have a real go at them, once and for all. You'd like that, wouldn't you?'

'I don't give a damn. They do their job. We do ours.'

'Oh,' he said, holding his hands up. 'Couldn't be better! You'll come out super. All the cabbies we've got so far are terrible, really shitty nasty people, accusing the minis of everything. If you come on all reasonable and intelligent you'll win hands down.'

'No thanks. I'm not typical. I don't intend to do it for ever.'

'But that *is* typical, don't you see? You're exactly what we want.'

'It's kind of you to ask me. But no.'

'It'd be £50, just for a day's filming.'

I said that seemed a lot, for a day's work. I didn't know the BBC paid such money. Joff said they didn't. Because it was me, he was putting it up quite a bit.

I finished my coffee, and the whisky, and moved to the door. I told him I had jobs all day and I couldn't let people down. We were short of drivers.

'I hear you and Eddie had a lovely meal while I was away . . .' I stopped. He was leering and smirking. My first reaction had been to blush, but as he watched me, I wanted to hit him.

He put his hand on my shoulder. I pushed him away. Come round any time, he said. Come round tonight. He was having a few people in. He knew there were several young people there I'd love to meet.

Drink, money, now sex. All that was missing was Green Shield stamps.

'Ok, £80 for the programme,' he said, quietly. 'I think I can just swing it. That's what we pay for Cabinet Ministers.'

I opened the door but he took my hand and said very gently, fine, fine, not to worry, he'd give me time to think about it. He was now trying the charm, but if that was the way he usually got people to appear in his documentaries, I couldn't understand why he'd been so successful. No finesse at all. He was probably the same in bed.

'One other little thing,' he said, pulling me back in the doorway and looking round to see no one was watching. 'You won't tell the police that I knew Zak, will you? There's a good chap. It would fuck up all my divorce again if anything like that came out . . .'

I ran to my car. In the distance I could hear him shouting £100, if he cut down on the others, he could just manage to pay me £100 . . .

That phoney policeman was more concerned about the point-less coincidence than anything else. He wasn't the slightest bit interested in the fact that someone had been killed and a family left fatherless. Mr Innocent and Co loved it only for the nasty gossip and innuendoes they could get out of it. Joff cared only about his name, his big-deal name, and what it could do to his own selfish affairs if he was known to have had any relationship with Zak. I shouldn't have run away. I should have asked him what that rela-tionship was.

After work, I put on my football socks, pads and training shoes as usual, then I went round to Sally's flat, running all the way. I should have gone to see her immediately. I was becoming as selfish as everyone else. Pre-occupied with myself and my convenience. I could at least take the kids out on the Heath. I could do her shopping. I could chat to her about Zak. There were lots of ways I could help. What a sod I'd become.

I'd admired Zak, really. He had strong views and principles, however crazy, and he stuck to them. He'd never harmed anybody by them. What's four pies to a wealthy chain of brewers? I was silly to let these petty things upset me. I needn't be so high and mighty. And what was wrong with Sally sleeping with blokes, even if she was married? Just because I didn't do that sort of thing, why shouldn't others? We got on well. We'd had a nice day out. She wasn't harming anyone. Zak must have known what she was like. He fixed her up with Shuggy after all. In this day of birth control, where's the wrong in it, for God's sake? There were several things I was ashamed about. I wasn't such a saint.

I ran up the stairs, trying not to pause on each landing for breath, counting between each floor to see if I could keep the same pace up all the way to the top. I arrived, choking, but without stopping. My policeman was standing at their front door. I had collapsed against a wall, sliding down it in an attempt to get my breath back. The minute I saw him I tried to turn and run down again.

'Surprise, surprise,' he said. 'She's not in. I thought *you* would have known that.'

He put his arm round me but I pushed him away. He was wearing a suede jacket and a black polo-neck sweater. I could see why they hated the graduate trainees, down at the police station.

'I was just coming to see you,' he said.

'I wouldn't,' I said, starting to run again. 'I'm out.'

'So am I,' he said, walking down the stairs again. My attempt at running was pathetic. 'Where shall we go?'

I explained I was late for football. He could come and see me another time. I'd told him everything I knew already. If he was waiting for Sally, he should stay. She wouldn't be far away.

'That's what I want to talk to you about. Sally.'

He had his arm on my arm again and I pushed him away. Another bloody toucher.

'Let's have a drink.' We were walking down the road, towards the Heath. 'I owe you one.'

'No thanks. Not before football.'

He stopped me in my path, standing slightly in front of me, putting on his grim, superior lawman's face. He was doing his duty. I had to help him. I hadn't got to force him, had I. Up till then, I'd never had any feelings about the police, either way. I'd had no experience and I'd discounted all the stories I'd heard. I was all for them, if anything.

We went in and sat down, in the private bar. He bought two pints and one packet of crisps, for me not for himself. He'd been very observant about my habits.

'You get good expenses, then,' I said.

'Not bad. How long have you been having it off with Sally?'

'I haven't.'

'Don't be silly.'

'I'm not.'

'Listen, we've seen a picture of you holding hands with her at the Cup Final.'

I laughed. I couldn't think what else to say. It was a pointless incident, sitting with her at the Cup Final, but too petty to deny. I asked how he knew that and he smirked, as if I'd admitted something very important. He said we could be seen in a two-second crowd shot. I was distinctly holding her hand. She had a long purple dress on. He'd been to the BBC and played it back that afternoon.

'She was passing me a Polo, that was all.'

'And the rest?'

'What made you think of looking?' I asked. 'Bloody Mr Innocent. He must have spotted us. What else did he tell you?'

'I'm not allowed to reveal my sources. Mr Innocent is one of the many people we've talked to about you. He's been very helpful.'

From his pocket he produced a letter, my little letter written to Sally, saying how sorry I was about Zak and offering any help.

'We found this in Sally's flat.'

'Liar. Mr Innocent gave it to you.'

'Now, now. Be careful.'

'So what does it prove? Nothing. I told you I was very friendly with both of them.'

'But you didn't tell us *how* friendly you were with her. Or that you spent the night with her, just a week after she was widowed. That's the sort of help you're offering, is it?'

'I didn't know at the time that she was widowed.'

'Would that have made any difference?'

'And I didn't spend the night.'

'A neighbour saw you both going in, hand in hand after the Cup Final. You were still there when she went to bed at one in the morning.'

'Listen, you've got it all wrong.'

'Put me right then.'

He thought he was so clever. I really hadn't lied or misled him in any way. He was misleading himself, yet he thought he had discovered something sensational, all on his own. The brilliant graduate mind at work, without using French, German or Latin either.

A gang of yobs had come in and were standing at the bar, pushing and shoving each other. The biggest one turned round and I saw that it was Vince. He caught sight of my companion, nudged his friends and they all started muttering and staring. Ginger was at the back, but pushed forward to have a better look. I could distinctly hear him say 'All coppers are bastards'. The policeman just smiled. He was above all that. He could take cheek, not like those old sweats on the beat who didn't know how to deal with the younger generation.

I wanted to get up and explain to Ginger. They obviously thought I was an informer, or even worse, a friend of the policeman. I smiled and waved. I leaned over and told them I'd see them on the Heath. I was just coming. They moved out in a gang, kicking over a stool, hoping to upset our drinks. Vince tried to knock our table, pretending it was an accident. That was it. They'd never play football with me again.

'I've got to go now,' I said.

'You were going to put me right,' said the policeman.

'What's the point, when you will get everything wrong. I can see why Shell didn't take you.'

He smiled again. He wouldn't let me upset him. He was above that.

'Ok,' I said, draining my glass. 'I did stay with her, till just after

one. It was the first time, and the last time. Just a one-night stand.
I'm sure Zak knew about it.'

'He was dead.'

'Bloody hell. You know what I mean. She often had other blokes
and he knew about it and didn't care. That was them. I wasn't
having an affair behind his back.'

'It might explain why someone killed him, though, wouldn't
it. Someone who wanted him out of the way. Someone who was
having an affair with his wife.'

'To you, it might. They were free and easy people. They did
what they liked. It wasn't that sort of scene. Ask Sally. She'll tell
you herself.'

'I'll do just that. And I'm sure she'll tell me exactly the same
things as you've told me.'

I wanted to hit him, to flatten his leer. I got up and went out.
He didn't try to stop me. I raced on to the Heath, but they'd gone.
There was no sign of Ginger anywhere.

16

They'd said there would only be one of them, but by mid morning
the living room was like a Tube train in the rush hour. Not only
had I been taken over, but the whole room had been changed
round. I was glad I'd persuaded Gran to go to work in the morning.
She'd wanted to watch and get involved, but that was the last thing
I wanted. She would have had hysterics at what they'd done to
her china cabinet and her chaise longue and all her other bits and
pieces. She'd had them all forty years, taken them with her on
every move, protected them through the Blitz and through evic-
tion. When I asked her to come and live with me, her only condition was that her furniture came too. Now they were piled high in
a corner, with an electrician climbing over them with big boots on
as if he was going up the front face of the Eiger.

I regretted ever having said yes. It certainly wasn't worth £100.
Joff had worked on me for a whole week. Even Eddie had said I
should do it. He'd popped into the office one morning with a note

from Joff, much to Mr Innocent's delight. He'd kept up the nasty jokes ever since. When Gran heard, she was all for it. She said I'd look lovely, and could she be interviewed too. She would take the day off work. Mr Innocent was furious with jealousy. He could see it all as a huge plug for Fantastic. He wanted me to wear a sweat shirt with Fantastic's address and phone number on. And, of course, he would be the real star of the show. I'd only been in the business six months. What did I know about anything? He'd spent a lifetime in mini-cabs. He'd tell them the real story.

I'd had a big row with Mr Innocent after the police visits. He denied he'd given them the letter, or that he'd told them about me being with Sally at the Cup Final. After a lot of screams and lies, and appealing to Sparkle as his judge, he agreed he had *seen* me on TV. I caught him out over Sally's purple dress. Sparkle remembered he'd come back boasting that he'd seen us in colour in one of the private lounges of the Hilton Hotel. But he hadn't given them any letter. Sparkle couldn't remember anything about any letter.

It was all rather stupid, with Mr Innocent shouting and raging and falling over himself as usual. But he changed completely when he heard about the proposed TV programme. He was all over me then. I took great delight in agreeing to everything Joff asked, as long as Mr Innocent wasn't involved in any way. I'd get my own back on him.

Joff was screaming at the researcher for having made a mess of some permission he was supposed to have got. Caroline, who looked even fatter in such a crowded room, was going round with bars of chocolate and sweets and chewing gum, as if they really were on emergency rations for the final assault on the Eiger. She had a stop watch round her neck and a big board in her hand and looked very professional. She'd been round every ten minutes with the rations, but I'd refused. I was in training.

Joff had made himself up four times, for each false start, with Caroline dabbing drops of make-up on and powdering the bald patch at the back of his head. I was the one to be interviewed, so I'd thought. No one had asked me if I wanted make-up. In fact, no one had asked me anything. This was the worst part of all, being ignored. I suppose I should have expected the chaos and the delays. I'd fondly thought they'd have been finished and away by ten o'clock. But with eight of them and all that equipment, there was bound to be complications.

They turned the lights on at last and I began to sweat. I asked if I could turn round in my arm-chair, to face Joff more. The director said fine, fine, however I sat was right. They just wanted me to be natural. As if I could be natural. It didn't even look my flat any more. They were poking things under my nose, taking readings, sticking microphones under my shirt.

They were all so worried and tense that I suddenly had the feeling that they weren't doing a programme on mini-cabs after all. I'd been tricked into something different. I was going to be grilled on my private life. They were going to prove that I was the brutal murderer of that innocent young man on the Heath.

The camera whirred, very noisily it seemed to me, and I sat staring at Joff, waiting for him to ask me something. He'd said it would just be an informal chat and he'd go over the points with me beforehand, which he hadn't done.

'Don't you think it's immoral,' he said, his jaw jutting out, 'and unfair, that someone like you with no experience, no qualifications, having passed no special driving test, having no special knowledge of London, unlicensed by any taxi authority and subject to no control by any local authority whatsoever and oh fuck, we'll do that again . . .'

I smiled, but no one else thought it was at all funny. There was panic all round as things clattered to a halt, everyone breathed in deeply, girded their loins, and started to tee themselves up once again. Joff was furiously reading from Caroline's board. She must have written out for him his first dynamic impromptu question. The director was trying to get a word in, whispering that perhaps, didn't Joff think, he should start quietly, work his way into it for a couple of mags, get the chap's confidence, and then, if he must, come on strong later. Joff swore at him. If he didn't like it, he could go back to Play School.

The first dynamic question was thrown at me three times in all. At the second attempt, the assistant cameraman fell over outside and an empty reel of film could be heard rolling all the way down the stairs.

I sat calmly, waiting for Joff to ask the questions. I agreed with most of what he said, so he was forced to take me through my life as a cab driver, how I'd got the job, had I had any fights with taxis, and did I ever solicit people. I replied yes to that last question, smiling at him. 'Don't we all?'

Joff was furious and shouted Cut. It wasn't allowed to involve him in the questions in any way. He was all manly and brusque and very BBC. He was the fly on the wall. I just had to talk to the camera. When we finished, they shot a whole reel of film on Joff alone. They turned the camera on him while he smiled, nodded, leaned back and forward, crossed and uncrossed his legs, looking belligerent, looking friendly and cocking his head to one side, giving his intelligent, thoughtful look. There was no sound running and he looked ridiculous. I decided I wouldn't go into TV after all. Mini-cabs might not always be legal, but they weren't phoney.

In the afternoon we did the so-called outside visuals, which mainly consisted of me playing football. They were very keen on this, a lovely change from a bloke talking to a camera in an armchair or driving a car. They'd teed it up in the inside interview, getting me to say what I liked about the job was the hours and being able to play football when I wanted to. They could then cut away to shots of me playing while I still went on talking about the driving.

It had been the researcher's job to arrange a match. I said I wasn't going to do it. He'd scoured the Heath and come up with an assortment of kids, cripples, sex maniacs and Ginger. They'd all been promised a quid a time to kick a ball to me and let me beat them in every tackle. Ginger was as amazed to see me as I was to see him. He kept on whispering to me, asking what was up then, how could he get in on this racket. It was the first time I'd seen him since being in the pub with the policeman. I was now back in his reckoning. He thought I must be a pretty big bloke after all. I said stick around. I'd see him ok. I'd explain everything on Sunday morning. I couldn't talk now.

It was six o'clock by the time we were finished. I had a terrible headache and I felt I'd been living with them for days. Then Joff decided there was one more question he wanted to ask, but it had to be done back in my flat. It would tie in with other questions, so it had to be done inside, because of continuity. I said sorry, my Gran would be home now. The crew said sorry. There had been one penalty payment already—for missing lunch. That was surely enough. The director said it was his kid's birthday. He was taking her to Oh Calcutta. Joff said hard fucking luck. We were going back.

Gran was delighted. She'd come home especially early, hoping to catch us. She had the tea on immediately and forced them to ask her a few questions to the camera, about what it was like to be a mini-cab driver's grandmother. The director explained to the cameraman that this would be strawberry footage. That was one of the many technical phrases I hadn't picked up.

The question Joff had forgotten was how much money I made. I said, quite truthfully, I didn't know. It varied, depending on how much I worked, the sort of jobs, the distances, the tips. He went on and on, trying to get me to agree to over £80, as he'd heard. Over £60 then. Around £50. I said the basic rate was 15 pence a mile and in a good week I made £40. But then I had the upkeep of my car, petrol, insurance, and the rest, but he didn't want to hear all that.

He started to make lots of snide comments about this lovely big flat, in the heart of Hampstead, surely I needed £3000 a year to live here, but I wouldn't budge. I thought about saying that Mr Innocent, working round the clock, made £80 a week, but I didn't want to give him any publicity. I had a good life, working the hours I fancied. I wasn't in it for the money.

I hadn't noticed that a ninth member had joined the crew, sitting behind them on the floor, obscured by Caroline, his back to me. He'd come in behind me through the open door. At the end of the reel I got up and I saw it was the policeman.

'I didn't know you were so famous,' he said, standing up and looking round at everyone scrambling to pack up. The lights had been put off and by comparison the room seemed to be in pitch darkness.

'Can't keep them away,' I said. 'MGM are coming tomorrow.

Sam Spiegel's been on the phone all afternoon. What do you want?'

I was showing off, which I was ashamed of, even as I was doing it. Going on TV had already affected me, which I'd vowed it wouldn't. I had been the centre of attention all day. I'd loved it, especially when I'd been playing football, beating everyone. Just like Match of the Day.

'What's it all for?' said the policeman, looking round.

'That's Jonathan Howard,' I said. 'Ask him. You know Jonathan Howard don't you . . .'

Not only had I been corrupted by my own self-importance, I was now name dropping, showing off my friendship with Jonathan Howard.

'This is Inspector Knacker of the Yard,' I said, all jolly.

Jonathan was very busy, going over with Caroline the next day's schedule. I could see him carefully ignoring me as we clambered over the cables to speak to him. He wasn't in an autograph-signing mood. He was looking our way, but staring through us, still talking to Caroline. It was his not-to-be-disturbed, I'm-too-important, face.

I thought to hell. It was my flat. I grabbed Joff's arm and said this is a police inspector. He's in charge of the Zak murder investigations. I wasn't sure if he was an inspector, but it sounded impressive and he didn't deny it.

Joff's words continued tripping out, fluent and aggressive as usual, bossing Caroline around, but a motor inside his head seemed suddenly to have stopped. Another had started up and was racing in a completely opposite direction. His eyes stiffened and his face went still. He took a step backwards, still talking to Caroline, telling her blankly where they'd meet, what to bring, what shots would be first, but it was slowly becoming gibberish as sentences were left unfinished and gestures stopped in mid air.

I was sure I didn't imagine it all, though I thought about it a lot later. I'd been watching Joff's face all day. I knew his mannerisms, when he was bored, when he was about to be clever, when he wasn't listening. Caroline was making notes, unaware of the change in Joff. The crew were banging down the stairs. The policeman was nosing round, picking up empty film spools. I was the only one watching Joff.

I think for once Joff was grateful that someone didn't know his name. My Inspector muttered something about not watching TV. Joff got his jacket on quickly, picked up his document case, told Caroline that she needn't drive him home and was off down the stairs before Gran could get his autograph. She was clutching three autograph books, from women in her department, just in case she'd see Joff in the flesh. She ran after him down the stairs, but he'd disappeared.

It seemed very empty when they'd all gone. Gran was twittering on about what a lovely man Mr Howard was. She didn't notice the marks on the furniture or that things had not been put back in their proper place.

The Inspector sat on the chaise longue, nodding away to Gran. I think she took him to be a member of the crew, who'd stayed on for some reason. I tried to get rid of him but Gran was forcing tea on him, asking him if he thought she'd be good on TV. He said she'd be a natural. He was sure of it.

'He's a policeman, you idiot,' I whispered loudly to her.

'Then what's he doing here?' she said, outraged at having been tricked.

The Inspector stood up and said he'd like a few words with me alone. Could we go somewhere, the station if I liked. Gran said she'd go to her room as she wasn't wanted, although why a TV man wanted to talk to me alone she didn't know.

I didn't offer him any beer this time. I'd had enough of him. Gran had already overdone it with the tea. He was poking round the room as if he owned the place, or had a search warrant.

'How's it going, then?' I said.

'Rotten,' he said.

'Get a proper job. Quit the police department.'

'I know that song as well,' he said. 'Quite amusing, but it doesn't make sense. "Sunday's on the phone to Monday. Monday's on the phone to you, oh yeah." Or something. It's just Paul trying to do a John.'

'You're quite a hip policeman.'

'We try our best,' he said, standing at the mantelpiece. 'Is this your make-up?'

He was holding Caroline's compact, the one she'd been using for Joff.

'No, it's not my shade,' I said flatly.

'Your grandmother's?' He was sniffing it. It was Mary Quant, with a big flower on it. Not exactly Gran's style, as even he could tell.

'Try some,' I said. 'You've got a few crows' feet you could do without. And those grey highlights are coming on strong. You want to tint them up. Could be very distinguished. You'd be a Superintendent right away.'

'We still can't find Zak's clothes,' he said, sitting down. 'Any idea where they might be?'

'Search me,' I said. 'As long as you don't tickle.'

He'd started the camp jokes. As usual, I was rising to the bait, knowing he'd probably take them as being serious, despite all his knowing remarks.

'But we think we're getting near a motive.'

'I am pleased.'

'He was queer, wasn't he?'

'I don't know,' I said. 'They say that about everybody these days.'

'And he fell out with his boy friend. It's always happening.'

'So you're not worried any more about me laying his wife? Or murdering him to get him out of the way and other sunny stories?'

'I didn't say that. But it does explain why he wasn't worried about his wife sleeping with blokes. The thing is, did he know that *you* were one of them? He might have thought that a real double cross.'

'You mean if I'd been sleeping with him, *and* his wife at the same time.'

'That would have upset me,' he said, frowning.

'But you are rather conventional,' I said. 'Having failed on the heterosexual angle, you're now trying the homosexual. Next you'll be saying I was his brother and it's all a bit of incest.'

'Fratricide.'

'Thanks. I wish I'd gone to school.'

He got up and started walking round again, lighting a cigarette. I got an ash tray, banging it down, to show I disapproved of smoking.

'You are homosexual, aren't you,' he said, stating it, not asking.

'No,' I said. 'Not more than you are. Less, probably.'

I felt myself blushing. It was such a bold question, a black or white question. When I thought of that evening with Sally, I had my fears. Not fears. What was there to fear? I had problems, that was all. But how was I to cope with them?

'There's nothing to be ashamed of,' he said. 'I was just asking.'

'I'm not ashamed,' I said quietly.

'So, you live alone with your grandmother. She brought you up, did she?' I nodded my head. 'You've got a very big flat here, as the gentleman said. It must cost a lot.'

'We both work,' I said. 'We don't drink, or smoke . . .'

'Or go out with girls.'

I stopped talking. If he was going to be silly now, I wasn't going to go on.

'I'm sorry,' he said. 'Undergraduate humour. I do apologise. Go on.'

'There's nothing else to say.'

He looked at me carefully, then he pulled a letter from his pocket.

'Perhaps you can tell me about this. We found it in your car.'

'Oh God, not another letter,' I said. I took it from him and read it. Somebody had been trying to get the sauce marks off and had made the writing even harder to read. I handed it back. 'You're not going to twist this one as well, are you?'

'It doesn't need to be twisted,' he said, taking it from me and reading it aloud, watching me as he did so. ' "Dear Franks. I'm sorry after all that I won't be coming to stay with you. It really would be better if I stayed here with Sally and the kids. It would be far too complicated otherwise.

' "Things are going well here at the moment. We've got quite a bit of money, although I know you think it's immoral to take it.

The trade figures are looking up and I might get something steady, now the summer is here.

' "The kids are well, in fact getting used to me at home. Tom said at school yesterday that his daddy's job was 'going out looking for work'. He thinks that's what all daddies do! Well, I'll come and see yous when I can get away. Love, Zak." '

He looked at me triumphantly. I didn't even laugh, it was so ridiculous.

'I know what "trade" means in homosexual slang,' he said, smugly, proud of his pathetic bit of knowledge. 'You didn't like him going off, selling his body to other people, did you? We've checked it's his writing. You can't deny that.'

I took the letter from him and explained very slowly, as if dealing with a child, that it wasn't addressed to me. It was a harmless letter from Zak to his Mum. Such a shame. He'd got everything, but everything, completely wrong.

'Firstly,' I said, 'it doesn't say Dear Franks. I don't know what it says, you've made such a balls of cleaning it up. It probably says Dear Folks. He was writing to his whole family.

'Secondly, the immoral bit refers to him taking dole money, not selling his body. Most good working-class families think it's shameful to take dole money.'

I went on to explain that Zak had intended going back up North, to look for a job there, but Sally had been against it. That's why he wasn't coming. As for the trade figures, only a wilful idiot could misunderstand that remark. The word "yous" should have been enough to let him see that the letter was addressed to a group of people. That was a common Northern expression, which even I knew. It didn't take a degree to work that out.

He didn't say anything. Just sat silently, staring at the letter, biting his lip.

'How come you've got the letter? In your car.'

'His mother gave it to me,' I said.

'Why?'

'Bloody hell,' I said impatiently. 'She just did.' It was a silly lie. I didn't know why I'd taken it, so why hadn't I said I'd taken it, for no reason. Anyway, it didn't matter.

'She sent it to you, did she?'

'No, I was up there.'

He then started asking why I was up there, when, doing what, why hadn't I told him before. I said he hadn't asked. He hadn't asked me a lot of things. He hadn't asked me if my Gran was in MI5, had he? It was his turn to tell me not to be silly. But I could sense that his theories were crumbling fast and that he was just snatching on to one little strand, clawing at it to save some of his pride. He said he would get on to Zak's mother right away. He believed me, of course. But he had to check.

'Actually, it was his sister,' I said. 'Or his Dad. One of them gave it to me. I didn't see his mother, now I think about it.'

'I see, I see,' he said, standing up, regaining a bit of authority. 'So you're changing your story now.'

'Get lost.'

I could see he was regretting that our relationship was informal and jokey. He'd started the matey chats. Now he was looking for a way of ending them and putting me in my place.

'He had far more money than he could have earned on the dole,' he said, standing at the door, about to open it, toying with one last thought. 'He must have been getting it some way. Do you know somebody called JB? We found those initials on a couple of things in his room.'

'No,' I said, refusing to think or help him in any way.

'You haven't received any presents yourself, have you, from someone called JB? Or anyone else? You look the sort of person people give lovely presents to.'

I went to the door and let him out without speaking. He had finished on a snide remark, just to annoy me. I was determined not to get upset. I actually wanted to help. I'd been a friend of Zak. I wanted the mystery cleared up. But if that meant helping that turd, I wasn't doing anything else.

I was absolutely exhausted. It had been the most strenuous day I'd had for years. But the worst part was to come. Explaining to Gran why the policeman had come to see me. She was out like a flash the minute he'd gone.

She was deliberately stupid, even though I went over everything, very slowly. I simplified a few things, not to hide anything, just to make it easy for her.

'He thinks I'm queer,' I said finally. 'That's the daftest part.'

She didn't say anything. She locked the door, pulled out the electric plugs and turned the gas off for the third time. I said what about our goodnight cocoa. She didn't answer me. It must have been the first time in our life together she hadn't made it. It was a ritual she swore by. She went to bed without a word, locking her bedroom door.

17

All week I wondered about being bent. Firstly, about whether I was. Secondly, whether everybody had always thought I was. It started by Midge coming up to me in the caff and saying 'Heh, I never knew you was like that. You know. Like that.' He wouldn't say anything else. I said I didn't fancy him, if that's what was worrying him.

Then Sparkle asked me to look at her tights, to see if I thought there were too many holes in them to go out dancing. She held up her dress so that I could have a good look, adding that she could trust me. Not like them others.

I blamed Mr Innocent. I was sure he'd been telling Midge and Sparkle a load of lies. They'd never have thought of it on their own. He probably told the police as well, telling them about me living with my Gran, having an expensive flat and other damning trivia which he'd picked up. He'd been spying on me all week.

He'd been furious about me going on TV and was determined to stir it up. Behind my back he'd gone round to Joff's house and asked if he could be on the programme as well. It would help his business so much. Just a few exterior shots of Fantastic's front door would do. After all, he did employ me. Joff had said yes, just to get rid of him and stop him snooping around.

All that day, Mr Innocent had been positioned outside his office in his best suit, cleaning the window, polishing his car, smirking at his own repulsive reflection, waiting for the TV cameras. With all

the delays and then Joff rushing off when the police arrived, there
had been no time for any more filming. Mr Innocent didn't know
all that, of course. He just presumed I'd stopped them filming him,
as a personal grudge against him.

He kept up the snide remarks all week, about if only he was
pretty he'd be on TV, if only he had contacts, and if only he got a
chance, he would help his old mates, not turn against them. I just
laughed at him, it was so ridiculous. If it was autographs he was
after, he should see my agent. Making jokes at his expense made it
worse, so I just tried to avoid him.

'Been to Jonathan Howard's recently, then,' he said one morning. 'Got a nice place, hasn't he? That Eddie's rather tasty, ain't he?'

'What do you mean?' I said, severely, deciding for once not to
joke it away, not to exit laughing, not to avoid it becoming too
serious.

'You know. A bit poofy.'

'How do you know he is?'

'Well he lives with Howard, doesn't he. He's his bloke.'

'What does that prove?'

'Oh, come on. I know Howard's married and got a kid, but that
doesn't stop them these days, does it? Sparkle knows, don't you?'

Everyone was standing watching us. Sparkle and Midge were
both there, not even bothering to look busy, lined up along the
office wall like an identity parade, watching me.

'It's like Zak,' Mr Innocent went on. 'He was married as well.
You can't tell these days can you. Not that I mind. Some of my best
clients are poofs. I don't mind at all.'

'Then why do you go on about it so much?' I said.

Mr Innocent laughed but I refused to smile. It was a joke to
him, a bit of harmless baiting. But not to me. I was determined to
see it through. Suddenly he stopped backing down the office, larking around, and stood still.

'*You're* the one who goes on about it, mate,' he said, quietly,
nastily. 'Not me. You're the one who's queer.'

He blurted it out, savagely, looking for a fight, self-righteously.
He was in the right and he didn't care what he said. Somebody had
to say it if he didn't.

I didn't say anything. Sparkle told Mr Innocent that he had a customer waiting in the car. He'd better go at once and leave poor Franko alone. I didn't like being described as poor. I didn't like being described as anything. But once you get described, denials only make things worse.

'And you better watch it from now on,' he said, lumbering through the door. 'I don't want my firm given a bad name. I know your tricks. I know what sort of soliciting you've been doing.'

I left soon afterwards and went to my car. I had no intention of leaving the firm because of him. It might just be stubbornness, but I wasn't going to be beaten by Mr Innocent. But I was sorry that Sparkle and Midge seemed to have turned against me as well. I don't know whether it was because of Mr Innocent telling them about my sex life, whatever that consisted of, or whether with all the police attention they began to believe I was seriously involved in Zak's death.

I went on the Heath as usual every day after work, in my training shoes and with my pads up my trousers, looking for lads to play with. I was hoping to see Ginger, but I couldn't find him. Every day I seemed to come face to face with the same people, their hair carefully arranged, carrying little bags with their towels and a spare costume, for sun bathing and other revels in the woods beside Highgate. The weather was now so warm that they were obviously out all night. They'd smile and walk ahead of me, or change direction suddenly, for no reason, and start walking swiftly another way, then stop, waiting for me to follow. I've always had a bit of that, in the streets as well as on the Heath, and it's always been a joke. If I've been with anyone, even Gran, I've laughed it off. But it began to worry me, frighten me even. It got to the stage where I started to run when I saw one of them coming. I was scared to look at anyone in case they thought I was after them. I asked Gran if she fancied having a dog, just so I could take it for walks round the Heath and look as if I had a respectable purpose. She said the only dogs she liked were poodles. I said no thanks.

I came back to the office from my last job one evening, all ready to go and play football, to find Shug waiting for me. He was sitting outside in a brand new yellow MGB, talking to Mr Innocent. He peeped his car horn as I drew up, opened the door and beckoned. I got in and made all the right noises, oohing and aaahing over his car. He drove like an idiot and I had to hold on to the door. He screamed at pedestrians trying to cross and overtook every car doing less than forty miles an hour. His hair was right down to his shoulders, but he said he was having it all off next week when training began for the new season. Probably get a skinhead cut. Long hair was out.

He looked tanned and mature somehow, a bit stockier. He was staring ahead, looking or shouting at other drivers, rather than me. I felt he didn't know what to say. I hadn't seen him for several months. He'd been on the club's close season tour to Spain and then he'd had two weeks' holiday in Majorca with Sammy. He'd passed his test first time, so he said, and had spent all his cash on the car. I said he wouldn't be needing me again on match days, to take him to the ground, but he said he would. Only the directors got proper parking facilities. With the players, it was first there first served.

He asked if I'd like to see his house, so I said yes. I wanted to ask if he'd come and play football with me on the Heath, but I was a bit embarrassed. It's like someone who can talk French being asked, go on then, talk French. He'd be so out of his class it would be silly. But I'd learn a lot. He would see how good I was, might even discover me. And it would do me a lot of good with people like Ginger. They'd really want to be in my team then.

The house had walls but no roof, and very little else. One building firm had gone broke, another had disappeared after he'd given them an advance to buy materials and he was now looking for a third. He was in a right mess. He had no more cash, as it had all gone in paying for the land.

'Do you wanna buy it?'

'What with?' I said. 'Bus tickets?'

'Come on. I know you've got a little pile stashed away.'

It wasn't a spontaneous, reflex remark. I could tell by the way he was watching me that he'd said it deliberately, as if he really thought I had the money to buy his house from him.

'You must be joking,' I said.

'No, really. I hear you've got a lovely pad yourself. I haven't been invited though, have I?' He laughed and slapped me on the knee. 'Luckily.'

I didn't know what he meant by luckily. He went on to tell me that he had fallen out with the club. He'd had such a bad drop in form at the end of last season, not scoring in four games and then getting into trouble on and off the pitch, that the manager was refusing to improve his contract. Nobody had put a bid in for him after all. It was all those rumours of him being worth £100,000 that had put people off.

'What have you been doing off the field?'

'Oh, you know. Turning up late for training, or not turning up. It's a waste of time most days. They're just bloody sadists. Then I was caught boozing at a club the night before a match. I hardly touched a drop. You just have to go into a place and they're all offering you a drink, shoving it into your hand. You can't refuse. It's the bloke you do refuse that goes off and rings the club. I got fined £50. We kept it out of the press.'

He started to explain their bonus schemes, but I couldn't follow it. Apart from getting extra for winning, for being a certain position in the League, for being in the first-team pool, they also had a complicated loyalty bonus, for long service and not getting booked or getting fined which Shug thought was diabolical.

'I've promised to be a good lad next season. They don't believe me of course. Thing is, all they do in the close season is argue the toss over contracts. That bloody manager never takes a holiday. He sleeps in the bloody stand I think. And they soon forget all the goals I scored last season.' He paused. 'So, let's hope nothing else comes out about me, eh, Franko.'

'You mean your sixteen illegitimate kids. Your LSD trips. Your two years in Borstal.'

'That sort of thing.'

He slapped me again and went all cocky, saying that Fantastic looked quite a nice little business. He might put a few thousand into it. Seemed a tidy investment. He'd been chatting up this Mr Innocent as he'd been waiting for me. Quite a nice feller, with lots of big ideas. He could do with a business partner. You couldn't think of these things too early. Sammy was such a con man he couldn't trust him.

I said I wouldn't trust Mr Innocent as far as I could throw him, and in his case, that was impossible.

'He can't help being fat,' said Shug. 'Poor bloke. And he's not well. Heart attacks, the lot. And all you do is take the piss out of him. He's got this very clever scheme with a chemical firm. Swore me to secrecy.'

'As he does with everyone,' I said. Shuggy would have to find out on his own about Mr Innocent. I'd thought he was hysterical at first, although it was hard to remember it now.

He said he'd drive me back home, no bother. He'd love to see my pad, then he said no, he'd just take me back to the office. My car was there. And anyway he might have another word with Mr Innocent.

'How's your Gran?' he asked. I'd never told him about my Gran, Mr Innocent must have been filling him up.

'Fine.'

'Does she know all about you and this murder case?' I didn't answer at first. I'd been waiting for him to bring it up. I knew he was going to.

'Of course,' I said. 'We did it together. I held him down while she poured boiling porridge up his trouser leg.'

'The police have been to see me,' said Shuggy quietly, ignoring my remarks.

He stopped the car and looked at me. I was surprised, but not as much as he expected. He looked very worried indeed.

'That clever clogs who went to university,' I asked. 'With the sidies?'

'That's right. He's found out I've been knocking off Sally. She says she didn't tell them. They'd found my telephone number in the flat and worked it out from there. I told them it was just a one-night stand.'

'That was all it was with me as well,' I said.

'You?'

Shug looked amazed. I knew now how far Mr Innocent had got in telling Shug about me before I'd arrived.

'The Cup Final night. Not bad, is she?'

'I don't know. I haven't seen her for months and months. If you see the police again, don't forget eh, it was just a one-night stand. The boss would be very uptight. In fact if I got mentioned at all in the case, I'd never get a new contract. He's shit hot on the club's good name and all that crap. You won't say anything about me, will you, Franko? Please.'

'What is there to say?' I asked.

'Nothing. You're right.'

We drew up outside the office. Shug leaned across and opened the car door for me as I couldn't work out how it opened. Mr Innocent was on the pavement, puffing and panting towards us, pulling faces, winking, waving with his hand. Out of the doorway came my Inspector, followed by another policeman, younger and more brutal looking.

I hadn't noticed them, but Shug had seen them at once. He accelerated away immediately I was out of his car. Mr Innocent put his arm round me, just to show what friends we all were. I pushed him away and went inside. The two policemen followed me. Standing against the wall, watching.

'Hello Sparkle,' I said. 'Buck House been on this afternoon?'

'Shuggy Gallacher's been here, looking for you very urgently . . .'

'I know, I know,' I said. 'So what else is new?'

She got up from her desk, smoothing down her hot pants, hoping the psychopath policeman was watching, and went into the cupboard at the back. She returned with two bottles of whisky and an envelope. Inside the envelope was a season ticket for next year, with love and best wishes from Shug.

'May I see?' said the Inspector.

'Why?' I said. I was fed up with being bossed about, followed and cross-examined by this know-all. Now he'd brought his keeper it was no longer a joke.

'Because I'm asking.'

'It's personal,' I said.

'It's a present from Mr Gallacher, isn't it? He must be very fond of you. People are always giving you little presents, aren't they. You must do people a lot of favours in return.'

'That's right. Now you do me a favour and let me get on with my work.'

'You've finished for the evening,' he said, smiling. 'This delightful young lady has just been telling me. She said you'd probably gone round the Heath, which you usually do every evening, after work. How interesting. What do you do exactly?'

'Play football,' I said, pulling up my trousers to reveal that I was wearing football socks and pads. Sparkle giggled. Mr Innocent hid his eyes in mock horror. Midge pretended to be working out dates on last year's calendar.

'Very kinky,' said the Inspector.

'Sparkle,' I said, 'any other messages?' I was regretting I'd told them the truth. I should just have been facetious and lied. I'd deliberately meant it to be funny, showing my legs, but they'd all laughed so much at my expense, as if I hadn't realised it was funny. I waited till they'd all finished laughing and then I asked Sparkle once again if there had been any messages for me. I was trying to be busy.

'A couple,' she said, clearing her desk for the evening and putting things away. 'Nothing important. Can't remember who. I didn't know either of them.'

'Well try to,' I said, severely. I was taking my bad temper out on Sparkle.

'I've written the names down somewhere,' she said, searching on the table but without finding them. 'It'll do tomorrow, won't it?'

'It'll have to, I suppose,' I said, wearily.

'As you have finished,' said the Inspector, 'and if you're not playing football, and if you're not going on any more nice car rides, perhaps we could have a word with you, hmm?'

The Inspector was beaming, trying to impress Sparkle by his reasonableness, yet showing off to his side kick that he was clued up and knew that he held all the cards.

'Sorry,' I said. 'I'm going home.'

'Well, we'll go home with you, won't we, Sergeant?'

'My Grandmother's allergic to policemen.'

'I'll tell you what,' he said, turning cold and nasty. 'We'll go down to the station.'

'No.'

'I'm asking you.'

'Hard cheese.'

'Such a school-boy phrase,' he said, managing to get a special emphasis on the word school-boy.

'Whatever you've got to ask me, you can ask me here.'

'We prefer not to.'

'I don't mind,' I said. 'Go ahead.'

'I'm just going,' said Sparkle, getting her coat.

'So am I,' said Midge.

Mr Innocent made no move. He was pretending to write out names in the book. I told all of them to sit still. They might as well share whatever jokes were coming.

'Have it your own way,' said the Inspector. I put my arm out to stop Sparkle, forcing her to sit down in her seat again.

'Your flat would have been the best place,' he said slowly and wearily, having such a silly boy to deal with. 'That's really all we want to talk to you about. It's such a nice big flat, rather luxurious really. Nice place for parties and meeting people, and for friends to use. I rather fancy it myself. Though of course, I could never afford it.' He gave a little laugh. 'Whose flat is it?'

'Mine.'

'I mean, who owns it. Who pays for it?'

'It belongs to a friend of mine,' I said slowly.

'According to the agents, the lease was bought by a certain J.W. Bates.'

'That's right,' I said.

'It so happens that the real name of your very close friend Jonathan Howard is Jonathan Bates.'

Mr Innocent was genuinely surprised at this. His belly started shaking, as he tried to get a word in, nodding his head and saying yes, yes.

'That would explain the initials . . .' Mr Innocent started to say, but the Inspector signalled him to be quiet.

'I thought that was just a joke,' I said. 'BBC gossip, that he'd changed his name . . .'

'You might think it's a joke,' said the Inspector. 'I suppose to you it's all rather a joke, having this flat paid for by someone else, while you pick up people and take them there, for their pleasure, and presumably your pleasure. I presume Zak and Jonathan Howard met there several times. I wonder if Zak was due to go there the night he was murdered, but didn't want . . . ?'

'Where does my Gran fit into all this?' I said. 'Was she supposed to be the madam? I hope you're making notes, Sparkle. My solicitor will have fun with all this load of gibberish.'

'No need to make notes, Mr Baxter,' said the Inspector. 'The facts will speak for themselves.'

'Zak was never in my flat in his life,' I said. 'Jonathan Howard came to it last week for the first time, purely for the sake of that TV interview. And as for J.W. Bates, that stands for Jean Wilhelmina Bates. She's commonly known as Billie and she's the owner of the lease. She also happens to be my wife.

'I haven't got my marriage licence on me at the moment,' I continued. 'But Somerset House would let you have a copy for a few shillings.'

There was silence. It wasn't much of a revelation, but it rather blew a factual hole in the Inspector's ridiculous theories.

'Billie,' said Sparkle, coming to life. 'Billie! Now where's that paper. One of the people who rang you was called Billie. She said she was ill and wanted you to come and see her as soon as possible. The line was very bad, but she said it was urgent.'

'She was ringing from Portugal,' I said. 'It's always a bad line.'

Mr Innocent put his head down again, going back to his books, trying to look busy.

'You're not *still* working, are you, Mr Innocent?' I said.

'Some bugger has to in this place,' he said.

'Good,' I said. 'In that case I wonder if you'd take me to London Airport. I'm taking part of my summer holidays from this evening. Drop me a postcard if you want me. My Gran will have the address. I'm surprised you missed it when you were breaking into my car and searching my flat. Don't do anybody I wouldn't do. Bye.'

18

I got to the airport, waited till Mr Innocent had gone, and then I got a taxi back. No one tried to pick me up. I couldn't see any mini-cabs around. They weren't all as smart as Fantastic.

Gran had a few days owing to her so I put her in my car and we went off to Brighton. Now and again, I can be rather master-ful. The only thing is, I go through a very long simmering period, when I'm messing around, undecided what to do, and then bang, I strike. I said we'd call ourselves Mr and Mrs Smith, just for laughs. But she didn't think it was funny. I'd done enough of that sort of thing already.

I rang Billie in Portugal but I couldn't get her. I left a message saying I'd been delayed, urgent work, I couldn't leave at the moment, but I hoped she was ok. I knew Billie. It was one of her tricks. She was always ill, putting it on specially to get sympathy. She'd promised I didn't need to go out till September. That had been the arrangement. She'd stuck to every arrangement so far and I didn't want her to start messing me around now.

We stayed three days in all at Brighton. I enjoyed the idea of the Inspector coming round to the flat to check up, and finding us both away. Not that he would. There wasn't much else he could ask me.

I went on a very strict health diet the minute I got back. I decided to use the holiday, however short, to get really in trim. I went for a run every morning and every afternoon I played foot-ball with Ginger. He was still on the dole and was grateful to have somebody else with time to spare. I discovered he was engaged, but he said it meant nothing. She was against him going out in a gang and getting into fights. I said, all innocently, that he didn't look the type to get into fights. He showed me his wounds. They'd been beating up a Pakki who'd hit back. I didn't make any com-ment. Ginger couldn't stand criticism or lecturing or people trying to improve him or help in any way. I said he was right not to get married. Only fools got married.

I wasn't foolish to marry Billie. I was stark, staring, raving mad.

It was on the rebound from Johnny, if you can call it that. I've never been quite clear in my mind what it was.

Billie used to come to the salon. She was the customer who always asked for me every time she came. It started with once a month, then once a week and finally every other day. She told me one day that she was going away on holiday to a villa she'd just bought in Portugal, but what would she do without me. As a joke, I said take me. Then I could do her hair every day.

In the crimping business, it's quite common to get invited to a client's house. I'd been up to the Hebrides for a weekend, all expenses paid, to stay with this titled woman. For a time it became the smart thing to have your hair stylist as one of your weekend guests, just to be around and look as trendy as possible. But with Billie, it had really been a joke. She was old enough to be my grandmother, well, my mother at least.

I'd been the only one in the salon who'd been kind to Billie. The rest were all very snooty when she'd come in the first day with her blue rinse and her Welsh accent. I'd knocked her into shape, given her a good cut, and made her quite presentable. I liked her because she was jolly and vulgar. She didn't realise that in a London salon, the hairdresser is the boss. The customers fawn on him, not the other way round. He's the one doing the favours. Which is why, like Johnny, it goes to their heads and makes them unbearable. They treat everyone like dirt, their customers and their assistants. They all hated Billie when she came bouncing in and called everyone pet, especially Johnny.

We kept up this joke for several weeks, about me going with her on her holidays, then one day she said she'd bought *our* tickets. I said she was mad. She said no. Come for dinner and she'd show them to me, and anything else I wanted to see. She opened her mouth and roared like a fishwife, startling everyone in the salon. Then she pulled up her dress to let me see her long knickers she'd just bought. They all stared round at her from their dryers, furious. Billie put her tongue out at them. I said yes, I'd love to have dinner with her.

Her Glyn had just gone and died and left her a widow and wasn't it all a laugh. He'd had two grocery shops in Splott which he'd sold just before his death for £50,000 and now it was all hers and wasn't that a scream. And did I know, she'd found these dirty pictures in his locked drawer, really disgusting they were, in fact she had them in her handbag if I wanted to see them. I said not during dinner. If only she'd known about the pictures. She could have posed for better ones herself, but the bugger had never asked her! Everyone in the restaurant turned round, amazed that so much vulgar laughter should come from one little woman.

'Now come on, pet. Don't be a rotten beggar. Say you'll come with me.'

All the lads at work said I should. They would go like a shot, if they were invited. Johnny said it was disgusting, taking advantage of her. I said he need talk. I honestly liked Billie. She so enjoyed herself. She was game for anything and would up and go anywhere or do anything, depending on her whim. Her whim had never had a chance, living all those years in Splott.

As for Billie, I told her I couldn't let Johnny down. We'd arranged to go on holiday together. He was big-headed and bitchy, but he was all right, underneath. Anyway, what would they think in Portugal, Mrs Bates arriving with a young single lad like me.

'They'll be bloody jealous, won't they. I'll tell you what then, pet. Don't be a rotten beggar all your life. Marry me.'

'Sorry, Billie,' I said, thinking of the first excuse. 'I'm queer.'

She collapsed at this. It was my funniest joke so far. But I wasn't sure it was a joke. Johnny was a bit like Joff in a way, taking anything that came along. He was trying to make me the same. I was sure it was the atmosphere that was doing it, the narcissistic work, the continual sexual interplay between the staff and the customers. It was all everyone ever talked or thought about. Once you get into that scene, it takes over your life, if you're not careful. Johnny said I was a puritan. Let it take over your life. That's what life's for.

'I don't care if you are queer,' said Billie. 'So much the better. You won't be trying to sleep with the maids.'

I didn't realise how serious she was till she brought a contract in, legally drawn up, whereby if I married her we would have two homes, the Portuguese villa and eventually a London flat. The London flat would be earmarked for my sole use. I could have it in any area I liked. She was already negotiating with an estate agent in Hampstead as she knew I liked that area. The only condition was that we should live together in Portugal for at least a year. I couldn't have the London flat till then. After that, it was up to me.

I fancied living abroad. I once tried to get on the Queen Mary salon, but I was too young. I nearly went to the Isle of Man once to be a croupier, but they changed the laws and it never opened.

'You're raving,' I said to Billie. 'You want your head felt.'

'And the rest,' she said.

'But ok, I'll marry you.'

It was a joke and it wasn't a joke. I felt I had to get away from Johnny, whatever happened. For several nights he'd come into my bed. It had been nothing more than pillow fights at first, wrestling, messing around, then he started playing with me. Eventually I'd let him. I don't know why. He said I enjoyed it. I said I didn't. It worried me all the time, the things he was doing and wanted me to do to him. I couldn't think of anything else. I was fascinated, yet afterwards I was revolted. One morning I'd wakened up with him beside me. The taste in my mouth made me sick. I said that was it. He said fuck off then. I was taking all the pleasure out of it. He could get someone else for the holidays.

Billie and I went straight out to Portugal after the ceremony. It gave her an entrée into local life which she would have found difficult otherwise, having a bloke. It was a bit of excitement for her and them, trying to work out what was going on between us. Her parties were hysterical. She'd told them one night that we'd met in a swimming pool. I was the attendant and she'd left her cubicle open. Then I'd been her skiing instructor and she'd come to me for private lessons. Or I'd been the barman who'd always put the it in her gin. In the geriatric, cocktail-belt parties on the Algarve, full of ancient ex-colonials, Billie was a sensation. They even believed her when she said she was thirty-six.

I loved Portugal. Some of the colonials were quite human, although I would have run a mile from them in real life. And I loved Billie, in my way, until I began to feel ashamed of myself. I rationalised it by saying I was making her happy. I hadn't beaten her up or gone off with her money, which is the sort of thing which could have happened to her, being so soft. Billie said I was being daft. There was nothing to be ashamed of.

Then I began to feel I'd given up life. I was becoming a cabbage, doing nothing, stultifying. I hated being so inactive. It was ok for the old colonials. They'd had their life. And it was ok for Billie. Her life was enjoying herself. I'm not so sold on merely enjoying myself. I began to realise that happiness is activity. At the end of six months, when Billie could see I was miserable, she said I should go back to London. She understood. She'd settled down now and had lots of friends. As long as I promised to come back and visit her every six months. That would be enough. I suspected she'd got a feller, a Portuguese creep even younger than me called José Antonio who wore white shoes and was supposed to be teaching her English. I didn't care. I was relieved if anything.

I felt ashamed most of all because I lied to everyone, even Gran, about Billie's age. Gran was so pleased when I came back that she never asked about Billie. Asking her to live with me was a way of forgetting Billie – and Johnny. Gran knew it was her flat, which she hated, but that was all. I was glad she never mentioned it. I'd felt sick with myself for marrying her, as I'd felt sick with myself so often when I'd been living with Johnny. I wanted to cut myself apart from both sorts of lives.

19

On the last day of my week's holiday it was hot, too hot for football but too cloudy to sunbathe, so I went for a walk on the Heath. I heard a noise at the bandstand, so I went across to watch, hoping it was a concert party rather than a band. Concert parties are a better laugh.

There were two lines of people from an old folks home sitting at the front, most of them mental as well as elderly by the look of them. They were hunched together as if they'd been poured on to the benches and left to set. A few had their backs turned to the stage and were waving at no one in an empty sky. But most of them appeared to be paying attention to the lady soprano who was struggling grimly through 'Some Enchanted Evening' accompanied on the piano by a man in half an evening suit.

Behind them were the kids, rows and rows of them, with parents and au pairs trying hard to keep them sitting down. They were fidgeting, asking when the funny man was coming back.

Further up the hill, on the slopes looking down on the concert enclosure, a gang of lads were lying on the grass. I recognised Ginger and Vince. They were throwing things at each other, now and again shouting or booing in the direction of the concert, but half-heartedly, knowing it wasn't really worth disrupting. There were two girls with them, dressed in the same black Crombie coats and with short hair, back and sides.

Ginger was telling some story to the girls, his head down, his eyes watching them. They were chewing gum and watching him contemptuously, giving nothing away, curling their lips. Now and again they burst into a loud raucous screech of laughter and turned away from him and made faces at each other while the rest of the lads cheered and applauded.

The singer finished and the funny man reappeared to the delight of the first two rows and the children behind. He had just started a series of Backing Britain jokes, to the murmurings from the children asking their parents what that meant, when down the central aisle came a group of ten people, dressed identically all in black. I hadn't noticed them arriving.

They were walking round and round the audience and as I watched them I could see that they weren't in identical uniforms after all. It was simply that their clothes all happened to be black – black shoes, black trousers, black polo necks. They held hands tightly in a line, protecting two of their number, a boy and a girl, who were struggling in the middle. The girl was shouting No, No, No. Save me.

The front two rows turned round to watch. Another treat laid on for their afternoon's entertainment. Most of the mothers tut-tutted, muttering that it was disgusting, where were the park keepers, telling their children to turn round at once, louts shouldn't be allowed to interrupt a concert. The couples at the back smiled at each other, convinced it was part of the concert.

The ten in black came to a halt at the side of the stage, clearing a way amongst the kids who'd escaped their keepers and managed to get a seat on the grass. The couple in the middle shouted louder and louder, putting on the screams and the agony, both now saying, No, No, No, Save me. The comedian shouted back at them but was ignored by the ten in black and by the audience. He stamped off the stage, leaving the pianist to continue until the disruption had finished. The pianist played a selection from *South Pacific*. Playing in open-air concerts in London Parks you have to get used to interruptions.

One of the ten turned to face the couple who were shouting, holding a book in his hand. He had a white dog collar round his neck which I hadn't noticed before. He told them to shut up, asking two of the others to hold them tight. Ignoring their continued shouts and screams, he started to recite the marriage ceremony. Do you take this woman to be your lawful wedded wife? Are there any just impediments why this man can not be married to this woman?

'I love Mary,' shrieked the bride, struggling to get free from her groom, clawing at the air and trying to kiss another girl in black who stood just a few yards away from her, trembling.

'I love Brian,' said the groom, struggling equally to get away from his marriage partner and reach a boy in black beside him.

'And I love money,' said the vicar, forcing them to come together. He grabbed each by the hand and held them roughly, making them be united while he continued with the ceremony.

Mary and Brian and the others in black all took up the wail of the couple being married, shouting that it was a sin, screaming that it was unfair, why couldn't people be free to marry anyone they liked. The vicar and his two henchmen kept tight hold of the couple, but at last they broke free, running to kiss their respective true loves. The two boys kissed each other passionately on the lips. The two girls flung their arms round each other. The rest of the group watched silently. Then the vicar strong-armed them back again and finished off the ceremony to the sobs and yells of the company.

Not one of them could act. Their performance had been embarrassing. They were like children in a very bad Christmas play, over-doing everything, shouting at the wrong moments, stilted and unnatural, hamming up the emotion, watching each other for cues and then getting it all wrong.

Yet I found it compelling. They'd put everything into it, carried away by their own excitement and intensity, unable to stop themselves, unaware of how it appeared to an outsider. Despite the noise and violence of it all, the effect had been gentle and fragile. They were so vulnerable, exposing themselves so openly, tempting derision and cruelty.

There was a pause while they rearranged themselves. Some of the couples who'd been standing at the back of the enclosure walked away, refusing to watch any more. Two elderly ladies from the front started clapping but were shushed into silence by their friends. Ginger and the lads on the slopes started to come nearer, wondering what had happened, getting ready to jeer and break it up.

The tallest of the group in black stepped into the middle of the circle, pretending he was interrupting them, the voice of the ordinary man saying his piece. He wore a blond wig and heavy blue eye shadow, but I could see at once that it was Eddie.

The lads at the back jeered but their girls told them to belt up. Eddie raised his right arm and started declaiming. People of all colours, of all creeds, of all sexes must be free. Majorities should not be allowed to persecute minorities. Remember what Marx said about the poor. They were oppressed. Everywhere minorities were in chains. He was hesitant and incoherent, neither finishing sentences nor developing ideas. Like all the demonstrators, Eddie appeared almost possessed.

The lads at the back were talking amongst themselves, egging each other on to start something. Parents were trying to get their children to turn round and face the stage again. Only the two front rows from the old folks home were loving every minute of it. They clapped for more.

Eddie suddenly came to an abrupt halt, finishing his speech in mid-sentence. Perhaps he realised that the yobs were about to make trouble and he'd decided after all not to be a martyr, or perhaps he'd come to the rehearsed end of their demonstration and he couldn't think of anything else to say. He smiled at the crowd and bowed his head. Then he raised himself again and asked everyone to join in.

'WHAT DO WE WANT?' Eddie shouted.

'WE WANT A GEE,' they all shouted back at him, holding hands and beaming.

'THEN GIVE ME A GEE! GIVE ME AN A! GIVE ME A Y. GAY!'

They finished their replies on a huge shout, then they held hands and moved slowly out of the enclosure, through the fence and up the hill and into the trees.

The pianist had been struggling on in the background with *Lilac Time*. He started a drum roll to attract attention and the comedian re-appeared. The concert resumed and the children settled down again. The yobs went back to sitting on the grass. I went up the hill to see where Eddie and the demonstrators had gone.

I felt saddened by their performance and somehow very alone, as if I'd been the only one affected by it, as if I'd been the only one who'd seen it all happen. I got to the top of Parliament Hill but they'd disappeared. I walked down towards the road and saw them getting into a worn and beat-up Dormobile.

It must take courage to do what they'd just done, but at least they were in a group, which must help, with each other for support. The same could probably be said for Ginger and the skinheads. On their own, they probably would never dare shout or interrupt anyone. But in a gang they were prepared to break up anything. But this time the skinheads hadn't been violent, just hanging idly around, looking for something to do.

I'd noticed with Eddie when he was walking away that he was sweating, as if he'd been through a violent bout of physical activity.

I'd never expected it of Eddie. Perhaps Joff, as a posture. No, on second thoughts, Joff would never have done that. He was much too concerned about his image. I admired Eddie. He obviously had the courage to stand up and be counted. It was a pity I didn't have more courage.

20

When I got back to work the police were waiting for me. Not my friendly neighbourhood Inspector this time, but his side kick, the heavy. There had been another body found on the Heath on Saturday evening. He was naked and had been found beside the same pool, but this time he wasn't dead. He was in hospital, unconscious, with the Inspector by his bedside, waiting for him to be able to speak. It was thought I might be able to help.

For once, I steadied myself before starting any complicated lies. I hadn't been to Portugal, as Mr Innocent and everyone thought, and presumably the police thought as well. I looked brown and fit and I hadn't bothered to tell them the truth. If I now told them I'd been at home most of the week, doing nothing, I would find myself caught up all over again.

'What sort of help would you like?' I said, throwing the question back at him.

'This photograph,' he said, producing an envelope from his pocket. 'We thought you might recognise him. Perhaps you've taken him to the Heath at some time.'

He had none of the leers and innuendoes of his superior. He was either thick or just going through the motions, knowing I had nothing to do with the body this time. I looked at the photograph. It showed a gentle-looking lad of about twenty-one, taken on a beach with his arms round another boy of the same age, both waving at the camera and larking around.

'We found this photograph in his clothes. He's the one on the left. Have you seen either of them before?'

'Nope,' I said. 'Never. Have you tried Mr Innocent?'

He said he'd tried every mini-cab driver in the area. No one could help. I said sorry, neither could I.

It kept the office in gossip all day, especially Mr Innocent. He seemed to be on the phone a lot, giving someone a running account of the latest developments, saying that no, he still hadn't talked, but it wouldn't be long.

I don't know why, but I felt he was talking to Joff. Whoever it was on the other end was obviously scared and Mr Innocent was holding something over him. Perhaps, once again, Joff had been on the Heath that night and Mr Innocent had taken him. I wouldn't put it past Mr Innocent to be blackmailing Joff. And as for Joff, I wouldn't put anything past him. In fact he probably knew everything the police wanted to know. I should have asked him months ago.

That evening, I decided just to arrive. Joff had always said I should pop in when I liked. There was always something happening. It happened to be a party. I made excuses on the doorstep, saying I hadn't realised, but Joff said don't be silly, come right in.

The main living room was done up like a sheikh's tent with silks and drapes everywhere and long cushions on the floor and people with hookahs lying down puffing away. I refused. Joff handed me a reefer. I put that down at once, as if it was dynamite. Joff laughed and told me not to be so silly. They wouldn't get raided. He had the police lined up. He knew too much about them. I sat for half an hour alone, drinking Coca-Cola, while everyone got increasingly stoned and increasingly naked. I felt like an official observer sent by Lord Longford. Joff forced some whisky upon me which I ungratefully took.

I asked where Eddie was, as I couldn't see him anywhere. Joff said he was out somewhere. He didn't know who with and he didn't care. He pushed another whisky on me. I asked if Eddie was ill again, was that the trouble. Joff gave me the bottle and said shut up. It was a happy party. He was celebrating his divorce. Drink up.

There were quite a few females I fancied, now I was getting in the mood, sitting giggling together, their belly buttons all painted, naked but for their bras and their long flowing transparent skirts. Joff made them get up on to a table where they all danced in line, pushing each other and shrieking at each other's jokes.

'Now girls,' shouted Joff. 'It's my turn. All close your eyes while I do my party piece.'

He went out of the room while the girls got down and lay on the floor, nudging each other, making eyes at everyone, anticipating in mock horror what was to come.

Joff came on absolutely naked. 'Look, I'm a man,' he said, standing in the middle of the room and grasping himself. He did a little dance, waving it at the girls who pretended to cover their eyes and look the other way, then he went out of the room again. This time he shrieked that he was a woman. He'd pulled himself between his legs so all you could see were his pubic hairs. It was the sort of juvenile trick the lads at school used to do when we went swimming at the Lido. I'd always looked the other way. This time I laughed. It was so childish and unclever, especially coming from Joff. A few straight-looking couples were standing in a corner, talking BBC gossip by the sound of it, ignoring Joff and his antics.

Next he pretended to be a dog, going round barking and trying to sniff people, lifting his leg beside them and howling. He then made a grab for one of the girls and tore her bra off. It was a boy. I felt stunned yet silly at not having realised. It must have been with living with Gran for so long. It was no doubt a normal London party. As no doubt Joff would tell me. He was now on the floor with the boy between his legs. I thought it was time I went into the kitchen and had a chicken leg.

What gets me about sex is all the energy it takes. I don't know where they get the strength from. I've met so many people whose sole concern in life is where they're going to get their next lay. I used to despise them when I was a young lad. But I suppose it's just like an itchy sunburn which needs calamine to cool it down. But was I missing something by not putting myself out?

Not thinking about sex is of course something you don't admit. I'd only ever admit to Gran that I'd rather have a game of football any time. Sex is over so quickly anyway. I'm asleep immediately.

But I had fancied those naked belly buttons, after a few glasses of whisky. When it's all around you, you can't help feeling you must be missing out somehow, which is the basis of all the adverts. But that's the stage I'd been through before. It ruled Johnny's life and eventually it began to rule mine. Much better to live quietly at home with Gran and have cocoa at ten o'clock and straight to bed. Or so I kept telling myself.

I had three chicken legs, several glasses of red wine and some smoked salmon things on toast. Most of the straight couples were

in the kitchen helping themselves, bored by Joff and his boys.
When the food began to run out, they started going. I got talking to one bloke and his wife. He said he found Joff's parties very
funny. He always had the same gang of boys along, rentapuff he
called them. They were very amusing, until they started falling
out. That was what often happened. Or Joff went too far and even
they were disgusted. They were nice kids, really, just enjoying
themselves. His wife made some coffee and told me her husband
was Joff's accountant. He didn't look like an accountant. She asked
what I did and I said I was in the Civil Service. When they left I
went back to see if the belly dancing girl-boys were now naked.
There had been quite a gang of them, enough to go round.

They were all leaving, standing in their street clothes, carrying make-up boxes and carrier bags. I never realised they were
so small. They were tossing their long hair, their coats over their
shoulders, like chorus girls going home after a bad first night. I
don't know what had happened. Joff was lying asleep, still naked,
in the middle of the drawing-room floor. Everybody else had gone
home.

Joff didn't say anything when he woke up. I started to move
away, but he said no, please stay. I went to the kitchen and made
him some coffee. He asked for whisky as well. I found I'd finished
the bottle. Joff staggered to a cupboard and opened another. He
poured two glasses and then went to put on some clothes. I waited,
sipping my whisky very slowly.

'What did you do that evening,' I asked, 'after Jack Straw's?'

He smiled, then waved his hands. He'd messed around the
Heath, the usual things he did when he managed to get loose from
Eddie.

'Did you see Zak?'

'No,' said Joff. 'There wasn't any point in seeing him, was there?'

'Why not?'

'I thought at first he was game, even though he'd have to be
paid. But he never did anything. All he did was roll people, take the
money and run away. I can do without people like that, thank you
very much.'

Joff had cheered up again. He poured more drinks but I refused.

I had to be going. Joff said he would come with me. He was going to look for Eddie. Perhaps I'd help him. He might be on the Heath. In trouble.

I don't know how we got there. The whisky had made me feel light-headed. I felt I could take off. I just had to turn the steering wheel up and we'd be in the sky, driving through the clouds. It was a dream I had a lot as a boy when I used to lie in bed ill with Gran rubbing my chest with camphorated oil and a yellow silk cloth on my back for its magical cooling properties.

We stumbled through the bushes with Joff going Sssh Sshh and then shouting and laughing, pretending to have discovered Eddie and someone together. Joff knew his way exactly, even in his state. We came to a clump of trees behind the ponds that I'd never been in before, despite years of Heath walking. There were flash lamps flickering under every bush and people standing talking in huddles, and then going off in couples into the dark. I could hear people falling and bushes breaking and people running, voices arguing and shrieking and others laughing and giggling.

It felt exciting. There was an air of adventure about it all. The grass was wet and the air was quite chilly. There were none of the luxurious comforts of Joff's drapes and thick pile carpets. We were out in the wilds against the elements, yet so swallowed up in the darkness and the excitement that nothing could really happen to us. It felt safe, whatever you did.

I thought of the war time when the sirens sounded and Gran used to pick me up out of bed, still half asleep, and we'd run for the Anderson air raid shelter in the back garden, clutching blankets and gas masks. I often pretended to fall down so I could lie there, looking at the blackness of London, criss-crossed with searchlights picking out barrage balloons and aeroplanes. There would be a deafening crash and a blinding light as a bomb exploded or the ack-ack guns hit the enemy planes in the air and they exploded above our heads. I loved every minute of it. I always wanted to watch it all. I screamed that I was safe. They couldn't harm me. Then Gran would pick me up, as I shouted and struggled, and take me into the real safety of the shelter.

Joff grabbed my hand and pointed to a line of blokes, standing just outside the bushes, on the edges of the action. He said they were the ones for sale but mixed up with them were the ones you'd get nowhere with, who were just after your money, like Zak. There was a certain excitement in finding out who was which, said Joff, if you liked being beaten up.

I asked him if he could see Eddie yet. I'd been looking everywhere. Joff laughed. You wouldn't find Eddie on the Heath. He'd just said he'd be here to make me drive him over. Eddie was too pure for bloody words. That was why they'd always argued. Joff didn't see what was wrong with being promiscuous. One-night stands did no one any harm. But Eddie was against all that, which was why Joff had to do it secretly, or when Eddie was away. This time, he probably wouldn't come back. He'd have to marry Caroline after all. He burst out laughing.

Then he took my hand and pointed to a gang of lads in the far distance. I couldn't see them in the dark but Joff said he could. He could tell by the way they walked, clumping in their big boots. Those were the lads you had to watch out for.

Suddenly there was a huge mass of light. Flash lamps pierced the dark and there were the sounds of shouting and dogs barking. There was a cry of Police and people got up from the bushes, still half naked, and started running.

I began to panic. I couldn't see Joff anywhere. He'd disappeared. I turned and started running, charging into the bushes, not knowing where I was going but determined to get away, anywhere, as fast as I could.

I could hear shouts and whistles as the police chased people behind me. I raced through the undergrowth towards the ponds, tearing my trousers, scratching my legs. I ran into the edges of a pond, the women's pond, and was slowed down by the mud and the water, but I dragged myself on until I was round it and into the open on the far side. I'd done nothing, talked to no one, but I didn't want to get caught by the police. I was frightened as much by the thought of a confrontation as by their dogs catching me. I couldn't be innocent when I felt so terrified and guilty.

At last, the shouts receded. I slowed down and began to pick up the familiar paths. I was panting, but not too much. I was grateful that I was fit and had been able to get away so quickly. Now that I was alone, every step I took seemed to echo. I stopped and waited, listening, to the Heath and to myself.

I got to the car eventually. The Heath had gone completely quiet. They'd all gone the other way. I had no intention of waiting for Joff and taking him home. He could look after himself. But he'd been very helpful. I knew now who to look for.

21

I got to Euston and put my car in the underground car park. It would be safer there than standing exposed in the streets all afternoon. I asked for a return to Stoke, the special train, the cheap-price one. I hadn't been able to see it up on the board, though the regular trains to Stoke were up in lights.

I went into the main hall and bought a paper and sat down to wait. There was no news at that time of the day, not that I expected anything. The boy who'd been beaten up on the Heath the previous week had come round but had refused to say anything. He said he'd fallen over a stone and knocked himself out. That was all. Not even the famous graduate Inspector could get him to talk.

There was the sound of shouting and cheering as some Liverpool supporters came off the Liverpool train. When they passed me, there were only six of them, looking round for the main party, but still determined to let London know they'd arrived.

As they got near the exit doors, a gang of about six Arsenal fans, waving red scarves, came in. They immediately started goading the Liverpool supporters, lashing out at them with their knotted scarves and trying to trip them up. Ginger and Vince were leading the Arsenal gang. It was all good humoured. No one was looking for a rumble. They were just acknowledging each other in passing, like two Silver Cloud Rolls drivers, saluting each other on the M1.

Suddenly there was a rush of feet and three policemen had grabbed Ginger and Vince and were twisting their arms behind their backs, forcing them to the end of the hall, bending them double, kicking them when they tried to lie on the ground. The other Arsenal lads were immediately subdued. They made a few protests, but not too loud in case they too were dragged away. They dispersed into the crowds then came out again, straggling towards the barrier for the train to Stoke. I followed them.

There was by now a big crowd at the barrier, yelling and shouting and waving their scarves. They were all aged about fourteen or fifteen. I looked around and saw no adults at all. I was the only one. Some of them were as young as ten, all dressed the same, plus a few girls.

I hung around while the others rushed down the platform the minute the barrier was open. There wasn't much point in going without Ginger. He was the reason I was going. Just before the train drew out, Ginger and Vince came running down the platform, yelling like mad. They jumped on the train as it was moving, with me behind them.

They were immediately surrounded and cheered by everyone on the train, the heroes whose story everyone wanted to hear. I sat down quietly at the end of their carriage beside two girls, thinking that would be the safest place.

The whole train was full of teenage football supporters. For the first half hour of the journey most of them hung out of the windows, shouting at people, throwing things and singing Arsenal songs. Ginger and Vince went up and down our carriage, sitting beside people, twisting arms, roughing them up. Vince was the one doing all the thumping. Ginger just nodded his head and smiled. Then they came back and stood beside me and began making obscene proposals to the two girls. Everyone climbed on the back of their seats and leaned over to get a good view, waiting for the action.

'Fuck off,' said one of the girls. She was as big as Vince with heavy shoulders and signs of a moustache. She was wearing a man's suit and heavy welted shoes.

'I'll fuck you,' said Vince.

'What with?' said the girl, spitting. 'I'll suck you in and blow you out in bubbles.'

Vince zipped down his flies and everyone cheered. He stood there, his hands at the ready, daring them to dare him.

'Do you want to see, eh? I'll frighten you to death. Nine inches of it. You got your ruler, Ginge.'

'Piss off, eh,' said the girl.

Vince threw open his trousers and displayed himself proudly, holding it erect.

'There you are, then. Tasty eh?'

Everyone was silent. The girls just stared at it, then looked away, bored.

'Fucking hell,' said one of the girls. 'Is that what all the fuss was about? I've got a bigger one myself.'

The girls bent down, doubled up at their own wit, leaning forward on the card table, their suits going up and down and their shoulders heaving.

'Put it away, Vince,' shouted a voice from the back. 'Here's old Bill!'

Two policemen, one behind the other, came down the passageway. Ginger and Vince sat down quickly beside me, pushing me along the seat.

'Two on each side. Out, you two.'

'Leave off of me, eh.'

'OUT!'

'We was here first. These birds have just come.'

'OUT!'

The policemen had Ginger and Vince by the ears, pulling them viciously, forcing them from their seats like lap dogs, then they pushed them out of the carriage, telling them to go to the end of the train, they'd find empty seats there. The police continued on their way, separating people and making them sit on their own seats.

When we got near Stoke, the singing and yelling out of the window began again and Ginger and Vince reappeared. The police were now guarding the doors, ready to stop any trouble-makers from getting off, their last chance of spoiling anyone's afternoon by making sure they missed the match.

The minute the train stopped, the supporters took over the platform, rushing forward as if they were at Dunkirk, storming the beaches, knocking everything before them. Outside the station they stopped and massed again, waiting till everyone was there, then they tied their red scarves at their belts, the knotted ends hanging down at the front, and they set off at a trot through the streets of Stoke. The lines of them, two and three abreast, stretched for miles. The local police were ready for them, indicating which way they had to go, lining up in front of any shop fronts which might be broken.

We got to the ground about an hour and a half before the match was due to begin, a careful plot by British Rail and the police to keep us out of the way of the normal supporters. Many went straight in, assembling at one end, hoping for a fight with the Stoke crowd, but they were on their own. The Stoke crowd hadn't arrived yet.

Ginger and Vince and the two girls went to a pub near the ground and I followed. I said I'd buy them a drink, being the older working man. The round cost me almost £2. There was a ten-pence-a-head deposit on all glasses, the barmaid explained when I started arguing. They did it every Saturday, otherwise the glasses got taken into the ground and were smashed over someone's head.

Arsenal won, which meant that after the match we jeered and laughed at the Stoke supporters all the way back to the train. At the station there was a big gang of Stoke supporters blocking the entrance, waiting to get their own back. Our lads stood their ground at first, eyeing them up. When the police tried to move everyone on, both sides booed and jeered. I saw a few knives appearing which I hadn't noticed before.

Our gang decided to charge, kicking wildly, lashing out with their fists as they fought a way through the Stoke lads. Many of them got knocked to the ground at once. The Stoke lads let them come towards them, then tripped them as they passed. Ginger and Vince managed to grab one Stoke supporter and smash him against the wall, blood pouring from his head. They carried on down the platform followed by about twenty Stoke lads, all ready to beat them up. Ginger and Vince ran round the trolleys and baggage, in and out of the lavatories, trying to hide. I heard what sounded like a shot then they were both on the ground with Stoke putting the boot in. The police finally caught up and separated them, dragging Ginger and Vince into an office and barricading the door.

I bought the girls tea and a fruit pie. We'd missed the supporters' train. The next train to London was in an hour and a half. We were being stared at by some schoolgirls, dressed conventionally in their weekend clothes, neat summer dresses and shoulder bags. My two girls deliberately did their worst, swearing loudly, narrowing their eyes, smoking hard.

They looked grotesque in their heavy double-breasted jackets. Each of them had a red handkerchief jutting out of their top pocket. Every weekend their mothers tried to get them into dresses. They'd rather die than wear a dress. They'd deliberately got jobs as messenger girls so that they could always dress like boys. There was something trusting about them. They wanted me to reassure them the boys were ok.

Ginger and Vince arrived in time for the last train, bandaged up and very proud of themselves, injured in a good cause. They'd won, of course. They'd taken on twenty of Stoke single-handed and would have murdered them if the police hadn't broken it open. The girls tenderly examined their wounds.

They were very quiet on the train home. A couple of stray Chelsea supporters similarly left over from their supporters' train, chanted 'ARSENAL SHIT, ARSENAL SHIT' as they squeezed past in the corridor but they were ignored.

We crept through Euston, a different species from the people who'd arrived to take it over at midday. I said I'd run them home in my car. I tried to cheer them up, saying what a good day it had been. But they weren't interested in football or Arsenal. It was the day being over which was depressing them. That was it till the next match. Back to boredom, to being forced to conform and do things when they were told. Worst of all, they had no money left. They'd spent it all going to Stoke.

The girls said to drop them at a Cypriot caff in Tufnell Park. They could get a cup of coffee there for free. One of the girls had a cousin who worked there. She said I could come as well. We sat there in silence for about half an hour, in a corner of a small dirty room, without getting any coffee. I decided I'd bought them enough. We all sat and looked at each other, chewing, sighing, doing nothing.

'Let's go and get some money,' said Vince.

We all got up and trailed out again, moving some Cypriots apart but not disturbing their conversation. We walked to the Heath and along Millfield Lane. They came to a line of cars and examined them carefully. I thought they were going to break in or perhaps steal them. They pointed out the neat pile of clothes in the back of one, a grey suit carefully folded. Vince got out his knife and slashed the tyres then we all ran away into the woods, the girls stumbling in their heavy shoes, moaning about their ankles. But there was action again. They'd come to life. They were walking faster, talking again, laughing and shouting.

'There's one of them,' said Vince. 'Come on. Charge!'

A man had come out of the bushes and was walking ahead of us. We got behind him trailing him, noisily, so that he knew. He started to run faster, looking round, very scared. Vince and Ginger jeered at him, smacking their lips, calling him darling, not to worry. All they wanted was his money, not his little bum.

He stopped, turning round to face us. 'You bastards,' he said. Ginger and Vince stood facing him. Vince pretended to hit him and he ducked and they laughed. He was wearing a broad leather belt with a big buckle. Ginger made a grab at it, swinging him by his belt to the ground. He made no attempt to fight. He was small and thin with a cheerful, open healthy face.

Ginger held him on the ground, his knee at the ready in his back, while Vince quickly went through his pockets. He pulled out a handful of notes and letters. Ginger let him go and examined what Vince had found. The man got up and ran away. Ginger and Vince were furious when they discovered they'd only got a quid. They shouted after him, but let him go, laughing.

We all sat on a seat, looking down the hill for anyone else coming up. I said there wasn't much fun in that, was there, one poor little bloke. Taking on twenty Stoke supporters was one thing, but taking a quid from a little bloke half their size, well, it wasn't worth it.

'They want putting down,' said Vince. 'All these fucking pansies.'

'What harm do they do?' I asked.

'One of them got my kid brother when he was seven. Dragged him into the bushes. I'd kill one of them with my bare hands if he tried it on me. I don't want some bloke trying to screw me.'

'Nor me,' said Ginger. 'We just want to stop them being queer. They need hammering. They deserve it. Bloody queers.'

I said they were doing it because it was easy, picking on people weaker than themselves who wouldn't go to the police afterwards.

'That's right,' said Vince, chewing. 'But if we don't do it, who will? Like beating Pakkis. Someone's got to get rid of them. We don't want them here, do we?'

'You're not doing wrong,' said Ginger. 'Not when you're hitting queers. It's not like thieving from a poor old woman, is it? It's like doing right, ain't it, Vince?'

They all nodded their heads, the Ku Klux Klan, virtuous and self-righteous. Then they burst out laughing. I asked them what was funny.

'It's all just a laugh, ain't it,' said Ginger. 'Something to do. You can't get caught. They like it, half of these pansies. So do I. You feel good when you put the boot in on a pansy's face. It's exciting.'

The girls said they'd hit one with a stick once, just the two of them on their own. It was easy. But the fucker had no money. They hit him harder for that.

It was getting dark. I wasn't sure if they were exaggerating for my benefit. But what I'd seen was bad enough. They'd have beaten up that little bloke if he'd struggled. I was trying to understand, rather than interfere, but I didn't know what I would have done if they had hit him. I didn't even know why I was still with them. I'd found out enough. I felt horrified but mesmerised by them, especially Ginger.

'Must be playing away tonight,' said Ginger, looking round.

'Probably all gone to Wimbledon Common,' said Vince.

'What we gonna do?'

They asked me if I'd got any money and I said no. I'd spent it all. They said liar.

'Leave him alone,' said one of the girls.

'Do you fancy him, do you?' said Ginger.

'Fuck off,' said the girl. Ginger grabbed her and they rolled on the floor, the girl fighting furiously, trying to grab Ginger's balls. He laughed then he got mad and rolled her over on her front, twisting her arm till she screamed in agony, the tears rolling down her face. He forced her to beg for mercy before he let go. She got up and said she was going. That was that. She stood on her own in the bushes for about ten minutes then she came back and sat down beside us again. We all waited in silence for something to happen.

'He's a queer, you know,' said Ginger to the girls, nodding at me. I smiled. I'd got to know Ginger pretty well in the last few weeks, so I thought. Even though I could never be one of them, I felt I'd been accepted, as someone on the fringe.

'That's right,' said Vince. 'So there's no use fancying him.'

I laughed and so did the girls. I'd played football with Ginger, got him on TV, bought him free drinks. I couldn't be queer, could I? I was his friend.

'What you laughing at, shit arse?' said Ginger. I still smiled. I thought he was joking, the way he did on the football pitch when he pretended he was going to thump some kid who'd made a mess of Ginger's pass. One minute he'd be furious, taking the game so seriously, as if the next goal was vital to the world, then the next moment he'd be lying on the ground, saying he was fed up, he wasn't playing any more, he didn't care who won.

'He's still laughing, Ginge,' said Vince, egging him on. Vince was watching Ginger with his bad eye, the one that was slightly crossed. Ginger made a grab for me, rabbit punching me in the stomach. I managed to push him away in time, sending him off the edge of the seat, but I was winded. The girls and Vince laughed at Ginger as he picked himself up.

'Think you're bloody clever, don't you,' said Ginger.

I knew I was as strong as him, if it came to a real fight, but I didn't for a moment think it would. It was the usual horseplay I'd seen all day, trials of strength between themselves when there was nothing else to do and no common enemy to fight. But I wasn't so sure about Vince. He had huge labourer's muscles and no sense of humour. There was also the girls, with their massive shoulders. I didn't know how much of that was padding or not.

'Why don't you piss off,' said Ginger to me, spitting on the ground. 'He's been following me for weeks.'

'He fancies you,' said Vince. 'Go on, give him a kiss.' Ginger gave Vince a push and then turned to me again.

'Go on, fuck off,' said Ginger standing in front of me. 'We don't want you sitting with us. Nobody invited you here.'

The trick was not to give in, but to brave it out until something else turned up. On the other hand, you musn't openly call the other's bluff. If the simulated aggression was laughed at too much it could turn real.

'Go on,' said Ginger.

'Fuck off yourself,' I said. It was the first time I'd sworn in years. But it was vital if I was to play my part. Swearing had to be answered by swearing.

Ginger suddenly went wild. He grabbed me by my battle-jacket, my new denim one I'd bought at Sid's Surplus Store in Kentish Town, especially for the match. I could hear it splitting. He was trying to pick me up but he hadn't the strength, which was making him more furious.

'Watch the material,' I said.

'You fucking pansy,' he said, bringing up his knee to hit me in the groin, but I managed to stop him. I lashed out with my foot, just meaning to push him away, keep him at a distance, but I caught him squarely on the knees and he went down, writhing in agony, as he did on the football pitch. He stayed there. I thought he was putting it on, but he wasn't. The girls were very worried and bent down to help him but he pushed them away, rolling on the ground, still in agony, clutching his knee. I could see tears in his eyes. It must be real. Very stiffly, I said I was sorry. I didn't know how you apologised, or even if you did. It was an accident.

'Let's have a look,' I said, going down to him, pulling up his trouser leg to see the extent of the injury.

'Get off,' he screamed, turning over and lashing out at me with his other foot. He caught me round the ankles and I fell to the ground. He got on top of me and we rolled over. He was screaming and scratching, completely wild and out of control, trying to kick and bite me. I didn't care any more about not hurting him.

He had no sympathy for me, or for that little bloke, or for Zak or anyone else he'd beaten up. He didn't care about anybody, when he thought he was safe and in a gang and picking on someone who wouldn't fight back. Trying to understand and be sympathetic had been pointless. I knew he despised me, probably had done all along. Violence was the language he understood. It was about time someone fought back.

His body was shaking and he was frothing at the mouth as we rolled over and over. I had to win. In the state he'd got himself, it was obvious I hadn't much chance if he managed to get control. He was all ribs and bones whereas I had the weight, but it was the one who could summon up most strength and hold on who would win. I felt I wasn't just fighting for me but for others, and for Ginger's sake as well. I subdued him at last, getting on top of him, pinning him to the ground. I wanted to make him apologise, the way he'd done with his girl.

'Get off, you're hurting,' he sobbed, banging his fists on the ground. He was still having hysterics. Letting him up wouldn't solve anything.

'I will if you promise . . .'

'Geroff!'

'If you promise . . .'

I didn't finish whatever it was I wanted him to promise. Vince had come from behind and got me by the throat. His grip was much harder than Ginger's. I felt myself choking, desperately trying to untie his hands. Ginger got free and still screaming grabbed me, kicking and punching my body. I felt myself going dizzy with being unable to breathe. All I wanted was Vince to stop choking me. Ginger's kicks were hurting but it was Vince I wanted to get off me. I took my hand away from his hands and went for his legs pulling him to the ground. We rolled over, with Vince still gripping my neck and Ginger kicking me.

Suddenly I couldn't fight any more and lay limp. Both of them were on top of me. I could feel blood trickling from my lips. My legs seemed to be broken. I looked into Ginger's eyes. He had an air pistol at my temple, the old-fashioned sort, with the steel rod down the barrel. I could see into it. There was no ammunition but I knew what would happen when it was fired. At that range I would get the full force of it. In the distance I could hear the girls screaming. Someone was coming. The police. I could hear dogs and whistles. Ginger pulled the trigger and I rolled over.

22

I opened one eye with great difficulty and saw my friendly neighbourhood Inspector. He wasn't looking at me. He was staring out of the window, unaware that I was no longer asleep. I closed my eyes again.

Next time I was awakened by rustling at the end of the bed. I sat up quickly, at least I tried to but I only managed to lean forward. It was like trying a new and fiendish Yoga exercise, putting myself in a position I'd never imagined was possible and then trying to hold it for a count of ten. I'd never be able to manage even the easy ones now . . . As for football, I might as well hang my boots up for ever.

The rustling was Mr Innocent's fat podgy fingers delving into a bag of grapes. They were going into his mouth like a conveyor belt, up to the tip, jerking, emptying, then back again. There were purple stains all over a brand new camel-hair coat. He had a white shirt on, a silk tie with a pearl tie pin.

'Hello, son,' he said, wiping his lips on a hankie. 'So what's the story?'

'I don't know,' I said. 'What year is it?'

'Late,' he said, pulling a bottle of Lucozade out of his pocket and another bag of grapes. I hadn't seen Lucozade since my Gran used to buy it for me, as a special treat, to improve my chest.

'How's business?' I said.

'Don't ask me,' he said, starting on the new grapes. 'What business?'

'Fantastic,' I said.

'We closed last month. I'm now an entrepreneur.'

'So what else is new?' I said, managing a Mr Innocent reply but closing my eyes as the strain had been too much. He droned on in the distance. He'd got contracts everywhere for hiring out vans to firms doing North Sea Gas conversions. All he did was stand back and take the money. He should have done it years ago. I wished him luck. I always knew he'd do it. Then I fell back exhausted.

He waddled out, leaving a circle of grape seeds round his chair. Then the sister came and put me back to sleep.

A bottle of champagne arrived the next day, followed by Joff. He'd heard about Fantastic closing. He'd come to offer me a job as a television researcher, a personal appointment, programme to programme, dealing with him exclusively, so that I wouldn't have to put up with any BBC bullshit. Now he was on his own, it would really be like being his personal secretary. I could even live at his place if I liked. I said no. He said think about it, think about it, he'd be in touch.

Gran came, to take away the champagne, with a message that Shug had been on the phone, enquiring after my health. In the first month of the season, he was already the leading goal scorer in the first division. He was definitely coming to see me. He couldn't have his old mate lying in hospital and not come and visit him. I said first division? Yes, said Gran. Hadn't I heard he'd been transferred? He never came.

I got a solicitor's letter from Portugal, plus a pile of bills and legal documents. Billie had died. Her illness had been real this time. The bills were all the ones she hadn't paid. I had to pay them by return of post. And if I wanted the body flown home, I had to come and get it. I tore the envelope up, and all the contents, then I fell asleep, crying.

I agreed to speak to the police at last. They'd come every morning since I'd regained consciousness but I'd refused to speak to them. They were shown in by the Sister. The Inspector had brought his heavy with him this time. I asked him to go. My eyes weren't strong enough for the sight of both of them. He went. It's great when the police are wanting you to help them. I looked at the Inspector, humming, my earphones on, spinning it out. If Gran had been there she would have said how rude. At last I put them down and faced him.

'You fell over, I suppose,' he said. 'And hit your head against a stone.'

'You've guessed,' I said. 'Now you've spoiled everything.'

'And presumably that little bump on the stone was enough to cause bruising and laceration of the under surfaces of both your temporal lobes.'

'Presumably.'

'That's the same as your friend Zak had. Only he died.'

'Bigger stone,' I said.

'Don't be silly,' he said slowly, getting up and walking round. 'You've got to tell us everything. I know how you feel. I understand. But there's nothing to be ashamed of. Some of my best friends at university were . . .'

I could see things so clearly. My head, now it had cleared, was translucent. I'd got everything in proportion at last. I knew where I was, what I was and almost what I was going to do next. Until the Inspector started.

'It'll go on happening, until you help us. Someone has got to identify them. We know them as well as you do. But we either catch them at it, or one of the victims helps us. You'll be helping others. Perhaps another of your friends will get attacked next . . .'

I don't know what it was, but everything began to go muzzy again. I was back to where I'd begun. The Inspector was getting it all wrong as usual, but at the same time he was basically right. Ginger had been baiting me, hadn't he? I had been hanging around him all those weeks. I didn't know why. I just did. It wasn't logical. I'd been waiting to be struck.

'If only we had more officers, we could patrol that part of the Heath properly. But we'd need about twenty to even start trying to do it. Changing the law hasn't helped us. It's brought out even more of them. Not that I'm against the law being changed. I don't mind what people do . . .'

I put my hand to my head. I asked him if he would go. I wanted to rest. He said of course, of course, he was sorry to have talked for so long. My health came first. I had to hurry and get better.

He came the next day and I refused to help him. I said it had been dark, when I fell over, and I didn't see anybody, when I fell over.

I didn't know why I wasn't helping him. It was stupid. He'd be confirmed in his opinion of me. But on the other hand, his opinion was partly right, which was why I didn't want anything in the newspapers.

I'd made a mistake, got the rules wrong, and angered Ginger. I should have given them money. It wouldn't help now for them to be sent to prison. Though there was Zak . . .

The police didn't come the next day, or the day after. I got up for the first time and walked down the corridor to the TV lounge and watched the children's programmes. When I came back, Ginger's Dad was sitting by my bedside.

He asked politely how I was and solemnly unwrapped a potted plant and put it on the window shelf behind me, then went to the sink to get some water. I asked him how Ginger was getting on.

Silently, he watered the plant, putting his glasses on to read the instructions, checking that he hadn't overdone it.

'We tried our best, you know,' he said, sighing and sitting down. 'We only did what we thought was right. We wanted him to stay in every night and study. We warned him against his friends, particularly Vince. That was a mistake. It just put him off us. Who else could he play with, living in that diabolical block.

'I used to think that Vince was totally bad. Now I know he's just like Ginger, half and half. I used to think Vince was the leader and Ginger followed. All parents think that. If their boy gets into trouble it's always him who's been led astray by some other boy. Now I know they're all the same. And it's our fault. We've failed them. We didn't accept him for what he was.'

I lay for a long time without replying.

'One of the girls has gone to the police. She's told all about Zak. They're questioning the boys now. I hope they tell the truth. That will be something to be grateful for. If and when it's all over, we might at least have something to build on.'

He sat silently, looking at his plant, as if listening to his forced sentences still hanging in the air. Then he left. The plant was already wilting with the heat from the radiator.

I left before the end of the trial. I had to go to Portugal to clear up Billie's estate.

It was rather lonely at first in her big house in the Algarve. Even though it had been shut up for only a few weeks there was a feeling of dampness in every room. I spent every morning sorting out her papers and in the afternoons I worked on the house, knocking it into shape. It was an old house, a converted sardine factory, and it had been because of me she'd bought it. When we'd first gone out to Portugal Billie had wanted a brand new whitewashed, red-roofed, concrete house with phoney arches at every corner. I'd said they were boring and stereotyped. They might be anywhere. What we wanted was an old house with character. But taking an old house meant that there were always repairs to be done.

The house led straight onto the beach which was the biggest advantage. In the evenings when the fishermen came in and pulled up their brightly painted boats I went down to see them. I played football with the younger ones until the sun went down. It became the highlight of my day.

When all the papers were arranged and settled and all Billie's bills had been paid, I found I was left with the house. I'd feared I might have to sell it to pay off her debts. I decided to stay on for another few months anyway. I dropped a note to Eddie, suggesting he should come out and see me some time. Which he did. On the next plane.

ALSO AVAILABLE FROM VALANCOURT BOOKS

Lightning Source UK Ltd.
Milton Keynes UK
UKOW04f0616040917
308541UK00001B/201/P